CALLED OUT

Praise for ...

CALLED OUT

Dara Nichole arrives on the inspirational scene with a page-turning novel that will leave you yearning for more! The characters are relatable, real, and refreshing; I couldn't wait to read about what happens next. Every teenager in search of a good book filled with true love, happiness and a splash of drama should read this book. You'll be glad you did!

—Kim Brooks, author of *He's Fine ... But is He Saved?* and *How to Date and Stay Saved*

Dara Nichole's debut novel, *Called Out,* is real, relevant and gives young adults a story that they can relate to by addressing issues and situations that they deal with everyday. This is a story that will not only give the young people the entertainment that they so diligently seek, but will also leave them with a powerful message. This tale of friends, family and faith is one that will resonate with readers for years to come.

—Monica Marie Jones Author of *The Ups and Downs of Being Round, Swag, Floss* and *Taste My Soul*

Dara Nichole connects with today's youth in a literary form that is both unique and inspiring. She combines youthful insight with mature life lessons that will captivate and retain the attention of the reader.

—Pastor Leslie R. Walker, Senior Pastor, Victorious Word Christian Center, Detroit, Michigan

Dara Nichole

Beautiful Works Publishing
Detroit, Michigan

Called Out Copyright© 2010 by Dara Nichole
All rights reserved
Beautiful Works Publishing, LLC

www.authordaranichole.com
info@authordaranichole.com
beautifulwords09@gmail.com

13 digit ISBN: 978-0-615-38149-7
10 digit ISBN: 0-615-38149-9

Cover design by: Marlon Hines Graphic Design
Book formatting by: Brenda Lewis/Ubangi-Graphics.com
Editing by: A-1 Editing Services
Make It Plain Editing

This is a work of fiction. Names, characters, places and incidents either are a product of the authors imagination or are used ficticiously, and any resemblance to actual person, living or dead, business establishments, events, or locales, is entirely coincidental.

ACKNOWLEDGEMENTS

To my God; my rock and my strength. Your patience with me has been amazing. I can't imagine my life without you. Thank you for what you have given me (on the inside), and for what you have done for me (molding me and growing me in your word). My mission is to convey your message to the masses and encourage them to trust you, like I have. I love you. **To my husband, Mr. Matthew J. Walker;** I love everything about you. Your support and love keeps a smile on my face. Thank you for supporting the gift that God put on the inside of me, I know you you are my biggest fan, and I live to honor you. I dedicate this to you. **My mother** (my supermodel), your strength and persistence inspire me, I want to be more and more like you Mommy! **My Father,** your quiet power is something that I admire, after all these years I still love to hear your voice say you love me! **My brother and sister, Carl and Rachel;** Thank you for being an example for Matthew and I, your family is beautiful. You are great parents! To **My mother and father in law;** thank you for being an awesome example for Matthew and I. Your advice has been priceless, and your words of encouragement are never forgotten. **To my core friends; Rhea, Ciara** (Happy birthday!), **Morgan, Nicole, Serena, Latrice** (Mommy!), **Stacie** (GG for life), **Kimberly Lovinlife, Daidria, Nikol, Britney, Ms. Cunningham, Mrs. Allen,** and **Joanna,** God has shown me that I honestly have been blessed to be able to call you all my "close friends." I know you all will always be there for me, just as I will be there for you.

Ms. Monica Marie Jones, I remember us sitting on the phone talking about writing a book, and now we are living our dreams! Thank you for always believing in me, and always supporting me! **Kim Brooks,** thank you for your constant encouragement, prayers, and support. I love you, and know that you will continue to be successful because of your love for God and your drive to please him! **Ms. Monique D. Mensah,** your advice has been golden! I appreciate the fact that as I reached up, you reached back to help someone you didn't even know. You personify sisterly love and support. **To the Fergusons;** You all have been there more than a lot of people probably care to know or understand, **Danielle** we share a special relationship that is so unique and ordained, and I know it will last through out the years of our lives. **To my church family, friends, family**

members, and co-workers, your words of encouragement, support and prayers have assisted me in producing my first novel. I hope you enjoy reading this, and I love you all.

Dara Nichole

CHAPTER 1

CALLED OUT

Thursday was always a hectic day: school, then dance practice, then homework, then whatever duties were given to me before 11:00 p.m. By the time I could relax, it was time to go to bed. Mom and Dad had it easy, though. Oh yeah, they came home from work; then Mom prepared dinner while Dad changed his clothes and plopped in front of the TV with a can of pop and a *Wall Street Journal*. It was never, "Well, Sweetie, I'll iron those clothes for you," or "Don't worry about the dishes tonight." I always had something to do while they did absolutely nothing.

"So Kiva, how was school?" my dad asked while walking casually by my room. He was a very handsome man to be a dad. He always wore those nice suits that seemed to fit him perfectly and, he never had a bad hair day. My aunt always said I looked like him, but I never saw the resemblance. He being 6'5 and I being 5'3, I just couldn't see it.

"It was straight; we talked about the Civil War and, yeah, that's it," I said dryly. Talking to someone I didn't want to be bothered with and wrapping my hair at the same time made me want to concentrate on the latter.

"Oh, well you know those leaves need to be raked and the den needs to be vacuumed, so when you're finished with your hair, get to business, alright?" He stood in my doorway loosening his tie, about to relax, and had the audacity to ask me, at 5'3" and 125 pounds, to rake the leaves? I just couldn't believe it. He walked away slowly, waiting for me to mumble, but after living in the Niran house for 17 years, I knew when to keep my mouth shut.

I plopped on my bed and slid off my boots and socks. As I laid back on my bed, I grabbed Mr. Squiggles, the first Teddy bear my father ever bought me. I was three years old when we went to the state fair and he won it by climbing the ladder and hitting the buzzer at the top. Back then I thought he was Superman, but now he's just Dad.

"Kiva, Sweetie, telephone," my mom yelled up the stairs from the kitchen. I knew who it was before I even picked it up. I turned my body over and scooted across to the other side of the bed and reached to grab the cord of the phone, which was dangling close to the end of my bed. As the phone fell I grabbed it just before it hit the ground. "Hello."

"Kiva, Kiva, Bo Beava, banana fanna, fo feava, me mi mo meava, ki..."

"Hey Monique, wassup?" I said before she could finish her sentence. She always knew how to make me smile, even when I was irritated.

"Nothin' much girl, just chillin' like a villain, you know how I do."

"Well, I can't talk long because I have to go rake the leaves before it gets dark, wassup tho?"

"Rake the leaves?!" Monique guffawed. "Isn't that why that strong hunk of a man you call your daddy lives there?" Monique was in love with my father.

"Please Monique, spare me the comments about how fine my daddy is," I replied.

"Well girl, when I see a good thing, I have no choice but to shout, hey!" Monique shouted over the phone like she had just caught the Holy Ghost. I could see her now, making that ugly face she makes while throwing one hand up in the air and the other holding her back. She was a mess, and I got all the laughs I could out of it.

"Well girl, I'll call you later because I have something to tell you about James." My eyes widened. James was the love of my life, even though he didn't know it, and I knew if she had something to say about him, it had to be important.

"I guess I can wait an extra five or ten minutes to rake the leaves; they ain't goin' nowhere," I said, holding in my excitement.

"Well, if you must know," Monique said sarcastically, "I was in line for lunch today and James came up behind me. He asked if you and I were going to Homecoming together, and I told him, maybe, but I didn't know."

By this time I was sitting on the edge of my bed. "So what happened after that?"

"Well, he said that his mom got a new car and he didn't want to go with his boys, he wanted a girl to go with, and he asked me who I thought wanted to go with him."

I jumped up and started pacing across my bedroom while waiting for her to finish the rest of the story. "So, what did you say?"

"Well, I told him that I didn't know and that maybe he should ask you who he should take."

"What! Why would you tell him that?" I fell back on my bed in disgust, trying to be quiet so my father wouldn't know I was still on the phone.

"Well Kiva, I didn't know what you wanted me to tell him. I figured it would give him an excuse for him to call you, and you an excuse to spend some extra time talking to him; shoot, I thought it was pretty clever," she said haughtily.

I sat up on my bed and thought about what she said. I guess she was right; now I had something to talk to him about tomorrow in school.

"I guess so Nique; I didn't think of it that way. Well, tomorrow I'll just talk to him at lunch, and—"

"Uh, you probably won't have to wait that long," Monique said nervously.

"Why is that?" I asked, trying to hold the phone and put on my jogging pants.

"Well, I kind of gave him your number; he said he was gonna call you around 9:30."

I sat there in silence.

"Alright, 'Nique, well I'm 'bout to get off the phone. I'll see you tomorrow. Watch your back," I said with an attitude.

"Whatever, Kiva, just thank me tomorrow when y'all are going to Homecoming together." I knew she meant well, but sometimes she just went about things the wrong way. I swear, if Jesus came down from on high and told her to go left, she would go right, just because she would have thought that she was helpin' him out. I hung up the phone and decided to get comfortable. I put on my high school hoody and reached under the bed to pull out of a box of old high school notes, flyers, pictures and invitations. I opened one up and was surprised to see who the sender was.

Hey Kiva,

    I saw you walking down the hallway and you dropped your notebook. I still have it, so if you want it, you can pick it up from my locker after school. Alright, bye.

James

After I received that letter, I thought James was the sweetest guy I ever met. The letter wasn't much, but it was something! Since freshman year, there was always something special about James Richardson. Now three years later, that something was still there.

When we were freshmen, he asked me to go to the movies with him, but my mom told me I couldn't go, so he took Shayla Thompson instead. They were together for about eight months; after that, I heard she broke up with him because he wouldn't have sex with her. So many girls tried to holla at James, and I see why. He's 6 feet tall, has dark chocolate skin, and just fine all the way around.

Nobody understood how I felt about James. See, to me his most important trait is that he is a devout Christian. He hasn't had sex, and as far as the rumors are concerned, he has a great reputation, and he goes to church faithfully every Sunday, or so I hear. That's what attracts me to him, that sweet, kind, loving attitude, with just a little bit of edge!

"Kiva, I'm not gonna ask you again, go rake those leaves!" My father yelled as he walked down the stairs. By this time, he had on a white polo shirt and some black swishy pants. I was so tired of doing chores.

"Dad, here I come." I grabbed my watch and my hat and ran down the stairs. It was 7:00 now; if he was calling at 9:30, I needed to be finished with all my chores and studying before I could settle into a pleasant conversation with James.

"Sweetie." My mother caught me right before I walked out of the door.

"Yes, Mom," I replied, turning around to see Paulette in a pink and white floral apron with white pearls around her neck and oven mitts on her hands.

"I wanted to know when a good day to look for your Homecoming dress was?" She slipped the oven mitts off and pulled out from one of her pockets a tiny notebook and a pen.

"Mom, I really don't know; how about Saturday afternoon?" I leaned against the door as she wrote down the date and time.

"That's cool, Sweetie. We can spend the whole day together. We could go get our nails done, grab a bite to eat. That would be great if—"

"Um, Mom, I hate to stop you, but I have to go rake the leaves and finish my homework. I am expecting an important phone call at 9:30, so I want to get everything done, okay?"

"Well, okay, go on out there and finish your chores."

"Thanks. Bye, Mom," I replied sarcastically.

"Bye," she said walking away and putting her mitts back on.

I loved my mom, but we were just so different. We never saw eye to eye on anything, not even clothes. So I knew Saturday was going to be a trip. My father and I were really close, though. When I was younger my mom had my brother all the time because he was so little, and I was with my dad, so I learned how to play sports, make model cars, and play video games, while my brother, at the age of 13, knows how to cook, play the piano, and sew his buttons on his jackets when they fall off.

An hour and a half later, when I finished raking and bagging the leaves, I stuck my head in the living room and asked, "Dad, where's Justin?"

"Oh, he's at the church and then he's staying the night over at Uncle Mike's. What's up, Princess?" My dad was in his usual spot, in the recliner with a *Wall Street Journal* in his lap and a cold Mountain Dew® in the holder. I walked in slowly and sat on the couch next to him.

"Nothing, I just hadn't seen him all day, and I wanted to know where he was." My dad looked at me and smiled. He then put his paper down and asked me what I wanted him to ask me all day.

"So, who are you going with to Homecoming?"

I slowly leaned forward and smiled. "Daddy, there's this guy,"

"Oh, here it goes," he said laughing lightly.

"Daddy, he's a really nice guy, he's really smart, and his mom is letting him use her car, he also plays—"

"Is he saved?" My father asked sternly. "Better yet, is he living saved?"

I knew that was coming. "Yes, Daddy. He goes to Blessed Temple, Aunty Deborah's church." I knew since he went to a church where family was, he would find it okay.

"Alright, just wanna make sure I don't have to school somebody."

"Daddy, he's really sweet."

"So, Baby Girl, what's the problem then?"

"Well, he hasn't asked me out yet, but he's calling me tonight to ask me about Homecoming, so I figure he's gonna ask me tonight." I clasped my hands together and ground my teeth at the thought of him asking and me being too nervous to answer.

"Baby, don't be nervous. And don't go chasing after him, either. In the Bible, it talks about men finding their women, not women chasing after them and clubbing them over the head. If he asks you and you feel comfortable, then say yes, but if you don't, then say no. I won't be mad at cha'."

"I know, Dad, I just don't want to say the wrong thing or do anything stupid." I got closer to him and put his arm around my neck. I felt for a second that I was eight years old again.

"Sweetie, God loves you and wants the best for you, so the only thing that you should be worried about is making sure that you are doing everything that is pleasing unto his sight, okay? Behave yourself accordingly and make sure that your body is continuously being used as a living sacrifice, which means no hanky panky. Of course you're going to be nervous. You were nervous on your first date, in your first dance recital, and even when you went to high school. Just talk it over with God and make sure first that this guy is worthy of pumping your gas. Then you will find peace and understand that Johnny, or whatever his name is, should be the one nervous, not you."

I sat in his arms and listened to my dad's advice. He was the best father I could ever have. He always showed me in every situation how God was affecting it.

"Yeah, you're right, Daddy. Thanks." I got up to go head upstairs, feeling so blessed because my father loved me enough to care about my relationship with Christ and always related it to my life. But would I know what to say at school tomorrow?

"Oh yeah, and Sweetie," he said right before I turned the corner.
"Yes?"

"Let tomorrow worry about itself, okay?" I laughed, nodded, and turned away.

CHAPTER 2

The clock said 9:29, and I was as cool as a fan cap. See, nobody knew how I felt about James but God. How I would daydream about our lives together and getting married, or when I would see him in the hallway, I would put my head down because I had such a big crush on him. Even the times I would go to the basketball games and root just for him. He was just too fine, and I couldn't wait to talk to him tonight.

I had peace about the conversation that was about to go on tonight. I felt special, even flattered, and decided I was not going to be nervous or worried. I was gonna let James do all the talking and I was going to do the listening.

I decided to clean up my room while I waited. I cleaned my vanity mirror. I turned on my radio but listened to some CDs since the songs on the radio talked about sex, drugs, or pimpin'. Who wants to hear about that all day, even if it does have a sweet beat?

I put in my Mary Mary CD and started dancin' to the rhythm. I loved everything about music—the drums, the bass, the guitars, the strings— if you put it all together the right way, it just made the sweetest sounds known to man. When you think about it, music controls the way we think, how we feel about things, and what we do. I remember the first time I went to the movies with my friends because Ludacris's new song was out and everybody was playing it at the theatre. I remember my first date because when I got into the car, he had "My First Love" playing, and from that point on that was our song. Music is therapeutic, it's mesmerizing, and that's why I have to watch what I listen to. Being a Christian ain't easy, but I sure do know how to make it easier on myself.

I was half way through the third song and making my bed when I realized it was after 9:30. As a matter of fact, it was almost 10:00. "He a trip," I told myself. I knew James was eager as they come, and he was gonna call; I'm not doubting that, but if he said 9:30, why hasn't he called yet?

I removed my makeup and got ready for bed. I had just turned on the TV when the phone rang. I grabbed it on the second ring.

"Hello."

"Hi Sweetie, this is Aunty Deborah. Is your mom still awake?" I looked at the phone as if it had betrayed me and yelled for my mother to pick up. "Aunty Deborah, are you gonna be long?" I inquired.

"Well, Kiva, are you expecting a phone call?"

"Well, kinda," I said sweetly.

"Kiva, get off the phone; you can use it when I'm done." My mother was on the line. I slammed the telephone down and rolled over. I really did not get along with her sometimes. She got on my last nerves. Seven minutes later, I heard her coming up the stairs, and I knew I didn't want to hear what she was going to say. I quickly turned over to watch my TV, but she walked in and stood in front of my television.

"Akiva Jeslyn Niran, I don't know who you think you are, but you don't slam the phone on me. Do you hear me talkin' to you?" She stood there mad, with her hands on her hips and forehead all frowned up.

"Mom, I'm sorry," I said. "Someone said that they were going to call me and they didn't, so I was mad."

"I don't care what you thought; you respect me and this house." Paulette stepped closer, and I thought for a moment she was going to hit me. Instead she sat on the edge of my bed.

"Look," she said softly, "I know we don't get along all the time, and we argue a lot, but we won't be able to get along until you submit yourself to my authority. I am the mother, not you. You don't question me or anything I say; I question you, okay?" She looked at me with love in her eyes and slowly kissed my forehead.

"Alright mom, I'll try."

"I will see you in the morning; you have a good night's rest, okay?"

I nodded. She walked out of my room and turned off the light. As I rolled back over to watch the *Cosby Show*, I thought about what she said. I was submissive to her. I did what she told me to do, and I heeded her commands. Maybe I needed to get a better understanding, because I thought I was doing okay.

By this time it was 10:15 and I was waiting patiently. I got up to go to the bathroom, and just as I returned to bed, the phone rang. I slowly reached over after the third ring and nestled the phone between my ear and the pillow.

"Hello."

"Uh, hi, can I speak to Akiva, please?"

I could tell he was nervous. "This is her; who is this?" I tried to play it cool, but on the inside, my stomach was flipping over. I could barely hold the phone.

"Hey Kiva, this is uh, James. How are you?"

"I'm fine; how about yourself?" I calmed down as I realized that he was just a boy, 17, just like me, and nervous, like I was earlier.

"Sorry I called so late. I had to finish my homework and do some things around the house first. So how was your day?"

"It was cool. After school I went to dance class and then I came home and did my chores, you know, stuff like that."

"I'm glad you had a good day. You know, Akiva, I was thinking about calling you all day. I just couldn't find the words to say, I mean, Akiva you—"

"Akiva, who are you on the phone with this late? It's almost 11:00!" My father was taking his usual pre-midnight bathroom visit. Those visits were the reason why I couldn't get away with anything because he was up periodically, checking on the house, looking in people's rooms, and doin' crazy stuff like that.

I sat up and put my hand over the mouth of the phone, hoping James wouldn't hear my father soundin' like a crazy man yelling through the house. "Daddy, I'll be off soon."

"Sorry about that," I was embarrassed and almost scared that this minor incident could make him reconsider asking me out or even talking to me.

"It's okay, Sweetie; my pops trips sometimes about me being on the phone late. But anyway back to our conversation."

With the mixture of slight discomfort and the melting of my heart because he called me Sweetie, I leaned back on my pillow and pulled the covers over my head, hoping that my father couldn't hear my incessant giggles when James mentioned how beautiful I was, or see the smile on my face when James talked about how much he loved everything about me. I was trying not to melt into his hands, but it just seemed as if we were meant to be. He was so sweet, so kind, and just the perfect guy.

"So James, I was wondering, why did you and Shayla break up?" He paused for a minute. I felt how uncomfortable it made him feel. I turned over in my bed and bit my lip just thinking that I may have messed up our conversation.

"Uh, it's cool. Actually Shayla and me broke up because she wasn't the girl I thought she was when we got together."

"Oh," I said with a smug grin on my face. "Well, I thought she went to church. Last year she was in the choir at St. Paul Baptist." I was hot, so I pulled the quilt off and closed my bedroom door. I sat in my huge rocker chair that my grandmother gave me five years ago. It had a cushion over the hard wood, and I covered myself with a cotton blanket.

"Yeah that's true, but it's not about what we can see, it's about her on the inside. See, Shayla was fake. She was smart and beautiful and goal oriented, but she just liked the idea of having a boyfriend. She didn't want to work at a relationship or get to know me for me. She just liked the attention.

"I feel you, James, but sometimes people don't know what they're doing and you have to explain to them and give them a chance.

"That's true, but since you weren't in the relationship, you really wouldn't know, now would you?" He sounded smug.

He shut me up. I sat there, contemplating what he said. I realized so much about him and his character at that moment. Being with someone isn't about what kind of car he has, how much money he has, or what he can do for you. It's more about who he is and what he stands for, especially in a relationship. It's deeper than we think, but what he just said opened my eyes real wide.

"So why did you and Michael break up?" He was almost laughing. I knew why, too. See, Michael was captain of the football team, about 6'3, full of muscles but no brains. He was so cute, and every girl in my high school wanted him.

"Well, if you must know, I was on that I-can-change-him tip," I commented.

By this time, James was trying to hold in his laughter. I smiled at all the times I got Michael to go to church with me, and then he would ask me to come over to his house, 'cause his mom was still at church so we would have the place to ourselves. I remembered how he would put his hands in my pants for good luck right before the football games. He was a trip, and he had taken me for a ride. I was so naive.

"Well, at least you learned your lesson, Miss Niran. I mean it's not every day a woman of your caliber dates a football player, and in the end gets to keep her clean reputation.

"I'm just glad I'm done with him, if my daddy ever knew everything that happened, Michael would be on the missing persons list. My daddy loves the Lord, but he crazy."

James laughed at my comment and sighed comfortably. "Why is this the first time we have ever been on the phone?"

"I don't know. We worked together in groups, and we've known each other for four years."

"Yeah, and you're still the same beautiful Akiva that I met three years ago, with that sparkle in your eye, beautiful smile, and kind heart. God is pleased with you, and you living for him. He is good, today, tomorrow and forever. And he will always love you, more than your mother or father ever could, and more than I could ever try."

I sat back and took in everything he said. "So you want to love me, huh?" I said with a smart mouth.

"I already do, but not in the way that I want to. I want to love you as a woman, one who can cherish me and my faults."

"Sounds like you looking for a wife!"

"Naw, just wifey material. I mean, why should I look for anything less?"

I sat in my chair with a big smile on my face. He was right. How was I supposed to prepare myself for being with someone if I always got with people who weren't worth my time?

"A big mistake that we make nowadays is getting with people God doesn't have for us, in your case Mike, in mine Shayla. We don't learn, we don't grow, we just stay stagnant. We as children of Christ, and me as a male, need to be looking for people trying to grow like us. I want someone who is trying to get everything life has for them."

"So what does that have to do with us being on the phone at 11:30 at night?"

"Well, I've been thinking about us, and I felt that we should get to know each other better, you know, shoot the breeze, hang out." He began to sound nervous again but with a little more confidence than before.

"I mean, we can hang; you have my number, and you know you can call me anytime—"

"No, what I mean to say is, well, it would be great if … I was just wondering if you would like to go to Homecoming with me, maybe?"

I almost jumped out of my seat. Mr. Richardson, or James to be exact, asked me, A.J. Niran, to Homecoming.

"Well, I mean that would be cool; sure I'll go with you," I replied very calmly. "It's getting late and you know we have to be at school by 7:15 a.m."

"Yeah, you're right. So I guess I'll see you in first hour then?

"Yeah, I'll be there."

"Alright, well, I'll talk to you later."

"Alright then."

"Okay."

"See ya."

"Goodnight."

"Goodnight."

I got out of the rocking chair, put the phone back on its stand, and fell into bed with my pillow on my face. I was squirming and screaming in excitement. Wow, God answered my prayer, even though it took four years. But hey, he's longsuffering towards me every day; I should be more than able to wait four measly years.

CHAPTER 3

W hat did I tell you? I knew it! You might as well thank me, because if it had not been for me on your side, I don't know—"

"Will you please shut up 'Nique, dang!" I hadn't had a chance to tell her what happened on the phone last night, but when James walked me from class to class and carried my books, Monique knew something was going on. "I mean we talked about a lot of things and one of them was Homecoming."

"Well, did he ask?"

"Did he ask what?"

"Girl, don't act stupid. Did he ask you to Homecoming, 'cause if he did, I have to find a date, seeing that it's in a couple of weeks."

"Girl, yes, he asked me; he also said that I was wifey material!" We grabbed each other's hands and silently screamed in the school library; then my cousin Kristen came over.

"What are ya'll screaming about?" Kristen is my cousin on my mom's side. She was wearing a red plaid miniskirt, a black long sleeved sheer top with a tank underneath, tall boots, a black belt around her waist, and a black fisherman's hat on her head. She was so different when it came to clothes, but unlike today, usually she was pretty cute.

"Girl, James asked Kiva to go to Homecoming!" I looked at Monique with a stare that could kill, while Kristen rolled her eyes at the thought of James Richardson even being in the vicinity.

"That Bible totin', verse quotin' boy that used to go with Shayla"?

"How did you know that?" Monique and I said at the same time. Kristen was a freshman, so when they were together she was still in middle school playin' kick ball.

"Girl, everybody knows about that. It's the only thing close to dirt anybody got on him." She plopped down in the chair and put her clear plastic book bag on top of the table. "But he is fine in his own, saved, sanctified kind of way." She smiled and nudged me with her elbow as if she secretly agreed to our date. "Oh, by the way, your mom invited me to go shopping with you guys tomorrow. Since I need a Homecoming dress anyway, I said yes." Just great, now I would have to deal with her mouth and my mother's all day.

I turned in my seat and looked at Kristen with an attitude. "You not taking that old man to Homecoming are you?" Everybody knew that Kristen was only 15, except for her boyfriend, who was 25 or "only 25" as she referred to him. He was almost old enough to be her daddy.

"Yes, I'm taking Oliver, and I don't see a problem with it." Oliver, or "O Boy," as he was lovingly called, had my aunt fooled. She thinks that he's 19 years old and that he goes to the University of Michigan, but who is 19 and drives a truck with rims and tinted windows? And don't forget the DVD player and television screens on the back of every seat. Kristen explained that in a mighty clever way. She told my aunt Deborah that Oliver's father is an executive for some big company and his mom is a college professor. They got a divorce and in the settlement, his mom got everything, including the car. But they don't live in a beautiful house because she said she didn't want anything that reminded her of his father, so she gave him the car that they had and she bought a Hyundai.

But wait, the lying doesn't stop there. Kristen told him that she's a junior in high school and that she's 17; she just looks young. The jury is still out on whether he believes that or not.

"Girl, Oliver is my husband, okay. I love him and I am not ashamed of him."

"Oh yeah, I'll make sure I'll tell him that next year when you just don't happen to graduate because of circumstances." Monique and I laughed and she looked at us and smiled. "How can you continue to lie to someone you say you love? If he loves you, he'll stay with you," I said sincerely.

"It's easy for you to say. You got a saint on your arms. I got to do what I can." She rolled her eyes and crossed her legs. For some reason, Kristen acted like she couldn't have a good man, like she had to settle for whatever came her way, which wasn't true.

"Besides, then I wouldn't be able to rock the house, you know what I mean?" She chuckled while we looked at each other and shook our heads. Yeah, Monique and me were still virgins, but Kristen said that having premarital sex was a part of life. Besides, she felt like God would forgive her because, after all, he was a forgiving God.

I used to tell her that she shouldn't take his grace and mercy for granted, and that sex is more than just a cheap thrill and should be taken more seriously. Granted I do get weak sometimes, but I have to stay pure, 'cause I don't want to miss my blessings. God is too good to take his mercy for granted, and plus my body is worth so much more than that. I mean, you don't let just anybody up in your house, so why would you let just anybody up in your temple?

"Anyways, Kristen, what kind of dress are you looking for?" I tried to avoid any sex, alcohol, or drug conversation with her.

"Oh, what, you not gon' preach to me today, evangelist Niran." She sat up in her chair and put her elbows on the table as if she was going to listen intently. I rolled my eyes and looked in the other direction toward the door. As I looked up, James walked in, right on time.

"He's here," I said with a big smile on my face. Monique laughed and started putting her books away while Kristen smacked her lips and folded her arms. He walked over to my table as I slowly gained my composure.

"Wassup Kiva?" He stood on the other side of the table and stared into my eyes. He looked so good. He had on some baggy jeans, never saggin', with a long sleeve black and red sweater and some tight gym shoes. His books were nestled in his right hand and he had a pencil behind his ear. When he smiled, all I saw were dimples and sideburns, and I could tell he had just got faded up. God surely was looking out for me.

"Hey James, I'm cool; you wanna sit down?" He smiled and rubbed his chin timidly.

"Yeah, uh sure, if I'm not bothering y'all." Kristen grabbed her bag and stood up quickly.

"Believe me, you weren't interrupting anything important." She looked back at us and walked away in slight anger. Monique looked puzzled, and I wondered what we did to upset her. I must've missed it, because last time I checked, she was the one with the problems.

"Well," Monique laughed slightly and shook her head while putting on her book bag. "I have to meet my mom after school, so I'll see you guys later."

I was so nervous. James sat down in the seat that Monique was sitting in and sat his books on the table. "Hello, Princess."

"Hey there, how was school?" I asked indignantly. That whole princess thing turned me off. Since my dad calls me that, it reminded me of him. I guess my dad knew that was going to happen; look at him ruining things, without even being here. That's Reginald for you.

"I'm cool. I'm glad I caught you before you went home."

"And why is that?" I asked, trying not to smile.

"Because I wanted to take you home. I know you usually take the bus or ride with one of your girls."

"Well, that's really nice of you, but I have to meet with my English teacher in like fifteen minutes." I hoped he would wait.

"I mean, I can wait, if you want me to." He was sitting so close to me, and I wanted to kiss him so bad. I started daydreaming, thinking about us and our children, when I realized he was still talking to me.

"Kiva, do you want me to wait or not?"

"Oh, uh, yeah, wait so we can talk about Homecoming stuff."

"Alright." He chuckled and took his pencil from behind his ear. "I was hoping I didn't lose you in your thoughts right there." I laughed and put my hand on his knee.

"Girl, you might not wanna touch me there; that's the hot spot. I might have to grab you like this." He picked me up and started tickling me. I was dying in laughter and asked him to put me down. He smelled so good; whoever put him on to whatever cologne he was wearing needed to be kissed. He put me down in my seat and I hit him lightly in the chest.

"You so silly, James; you play too much." He laughed and pulled me close to him. I fell into his arms and he kissed my forehead. I laid my head in his chest and listened to his heartbeat. We both pulled back slowly, not wanting to let go, and looked at each other.

"You know Kiva, I've been wanting to chill wit you like this for awhile." I looked away and he grabbed my chin to look at him. "Kiva, for real, man—"

"James, stop now. I know how you feel, and I believe you, but I gotta go, so can we talk about this on our way home?" I felt bad leaving him like that in mid sentence, I just couldn't be that close to him right then. He was soo fine!

"Alright, I'll be in the gym, so just come there after you leave Mrs. Ruffin's room." I walked away from him slowly picking up my books, and when I turned around I caught him looking at my shape. I was shocked, but not surprised; after all, he is a boy.

"Well, I'll meet you in the gym, and thank you for waiting." I smiled over my shoulder as I walked away. He grabbed his books from the table, rubbed his chin, and walked towards the gym. He was the most thug-lookin' Christian I had ever seen. See, that was the thing though, girls knew he was saved, but they saw that hardcore in him, and if he liked being that way, I loved it. Fine, saved, and sanctified, can't beat that combination.

CHAPTER 4

I walked into the gym after my session with Mrs. Ruffin to find three sweaty boys playing basketball. I should have known. By this time, James had shed the sweater and the bookbag and was in his T-shirt and jeans, like Alonzo and Nate, his roll dawgs. Alonzo was cool; we went to middle school together and had always been able to talk about old times. He was saved as well. When we got to high school, girls were all over him, and he slipped a couple times, but when he and James got on the Varsity team together, girls knew he wasn't goin' for all that any more.

Nate, on the other hand, was working on it. He and James got cool only because Nate was co-captain and Alonzo was captain, but Alonzo was always asking James how he should run the team. Nate didn't like that, so he told him how he felt, and after two or three weeks of arguing, they finally became cool. It's amazing how boys can just forget everything that happened and start anew, but girls will hold you accountable for stuff that happened in the fifth grade. We are so petty sometimes, but they always say we're more mature.

"I thought you knew how to play, man; you suck!" Alonzo taunted James as he was dribbling and getting ready to go up for the shot.

"Man, watch me dunk this right in yo face!" James had his game face on. Alonzo tried to block while James dribbled and somehow got around him to go up. He dunked the ball and hung from the rim in pride.

"Man, whateva, you just showin' off in front of the girls." Until that moment, I didn't realize that there were others in the gym. I looked in the bleachers and saw Natalie, Nate's girlfriend, and Shawny, Natalie's best friend. They both were sitting there laughing and giggling with their matching bright orange and yellow shirts on. They were both too much for me.

"Man, ain't nobody thinkin' about them," James said wiping the sweat off his forehead and walking toward me.

"You ready?" He looked at me like he hadn't seen me all day.

"Yeah, whenever you are." I sat on the bleachers next to his stuff and smiled. James was so fine, and I knew Shawny and Natalie were on their way down here to see what I was doing. As soon as I looked to my left, I saw Shawny wave at me. Funny how when people want to be all in your business they say hi, but when you're in the hallway in school and you smile, they look at you like you're crazy. I waved back and folded my legs and started watching them play a quick game of horse. After a couple of minutes, I heard the bleachers start to shake and heard their voices coming toward me. Everybody knew that Shawny was absolutely in love with James, so I really wanted to spare her the embarrassment.

"Hey, Akiva, did you get your paper back from Mr. Fentin? I wanted to know what other people got because I got a B, and I feel I should have got a better grade." I looked at Natalie and wanted to laugh. She was very fair skinned with medium length hair. Even though she always had it up in some kind of clip, it was always different. Shawny used to be on the cheerleading team, but this year, our senior year decided to call it quits.

"Um, yeah I got an A- because he said that I didn't cite my information correctly."

She sat down next to me and acted as if she was really interested. "So, who you waiting for?" She asked with a smile. I looked up at Shawny who was still standing on the other side of me looking very interested in my answer.

"Oh, I'm waiting for James; he's taking me home today." I sat up straight and tried to act as if I was paying attention to their game. "We were in the library and since we're both going the same way, he offered." They looked at each other and Shawny sat down next to me.

"Well, Akiva, he lives off of 7 Mile and Livernois and you live near me off of Grand River, so I can take you home. You don't have to wait for them to finish playing; they could take all day." Natalie had her nerve. I had forgotten that she lived near me, but I was not leaving him here so Ms. Shawny could take a bite out of my chocolate man. Did I say my man? Let me check myself real quick. Anyway, she wasn't slick, and I could see right through her.

"Naw Natalie, I'm straight; besides, don't you wanna stay here with Nate? I know you ain't gon' leave him here by himself." I looked at her straight in the face and smiled a sarcastic smile. She smiled back and rolled her eyes.

I couldn't stand her pompous ghetto attitude. Anyways, back to James. By this time he was sweating and had taken off his T-shirt. His chest was a dark chocolate, and all I saw was sweat and a silver chain every time he went up for a shot. I was ready to go; I needed to get into my prayer closet.

"Akiva, you ready?" He sauntered toward me. When he reached behind me to grab his towel, his arm brushed my shoulder. He began to wipe his face and chest and threw his T-shirt back on. I was through.

"Uh yeah, I'm ready" I grabbed my bag as he pulled his sweater on and we walked to his car.

"Sorry I made you wait; we just got in the middle of a game and I had to finish. You know how that goes."

"Yeah, it's cool. I'm fine." Deep down I wanted to throw him down. We pulled up in front of my house and sat there listening to commercials, trying not to let our hormones take us over.

"James, what color do you want to wear to Homecoming?"

"Oh, it doesn't matter. I like cream, though; if you find a cream dress that would be cool." All I could think about was his chest; the image of it was in my mind, and I just could not shake it. The devil was playin' with me.

"Well, give me a call tonight, alright?" I opened the car door, and stepped one foot out.

"Alright, I'll call you around 8:00 or 9:00."

As I walked to my house, I realized how much of a test this was going to be. Just being in James' presence was hard. And I heard that Nate had a hotel room for all his friends to come over and chill after the dance. Lord, I need you right now.

✝✝✝✝✝✝✝

"Can we listen to something? I really don't feel like hearing any choirs this morning." Kristen was always complaining about something. My mom decided to start our day at 9:00 a.m., which meant I had to be up by 8:15 to get ready on a Saturday; ridiculous.

"You fill your spirit with all that trash, and then you wonder why you do the things you do, or say the things you say, 'cause of that music. You need to stop listening to that junk." She was right; my mom knew her word, she knew her Bible, and she knew God. I admired her for that, but I just wish she knew me better.

"You can't even understand what the choir is saying, it's so many of them, I mean can we at least, just not listen to anything?"

"Kristen, shut up. You always got something to say. Here, I'll put in Mary Mary for you; they don't have any choirs." She looked at me as if to say, "You better be happy your mother is in the car," and rolled her eyes. So bitter and yet so young. We pulled up into the mall and got out of the car.

"Are you going in the actual store with us, or are you just going to give me the money so we can look together?" I asked. I felt bad after I said it, but I really didn't want her watching while I tried on dresses. The comment seemed to not faze her at all.

"Don't worry, after our talk the other day I figured you were gonna feel that way. That's why your cousin is here, so you two can go on, and call me when you're ready to buy it. I'm going shopping for myself." Once we got in the mall, Kristen quickly got on her cell phone after we left my mom.

"I know, that dude ain't s***" She looked at me and changed her tone real quick.

"I mean, yeah, you know he ain't no good. Naw I'm going over O's house tonight; we supposed to have the place all to ourselves 'cause his parents goin' out of town. Girl, you know it, strawberries on top of me." I couldn't believe I was hearing this conversation. My cousin was too out there, but it just made me feel like, dang, why am I waiting, it must be good if she can't get enough.

"But yeah, girl, I'm out here with A.J., shoppin' for Homecoming dresses, so I'll give you a call later, girl. I told you, she was my cousin; y'all just can't believe we got the same blood huh! Yeah, alright girl, bye."

"You are so rude," I said speeding up my walk.

"What you mean? It's not like you was in the middle of a conversation." She huffed and looked in another direction.

"Who was that anyway on the phone?"

"Yo' old nosy butt, you just wanted to know who I was talking to!" We both laughed and decided to get a Cinnabon® before we went shopping. As we waited in line, she told me about her friend, Nakiya, who was in her grade. Apparently the guy she was messing with was married, and her wife found out about them messing around. Of course, the wife and

Nakiya had a big argument over the phone and she hadn't talked to him in a couple weeks, but now he's callin' her off the hook to meet her at the mall tonight so they can talk.

"Well, is she going?" I inquired.

Kristen grabbed her Cinnabon® and looked me right in the face. "She's on her way right now."

I shook my head and sat down. Kristen could be real cool when she wanted to, but she was always involved in some drama and thought it was normal.

"You know you shouldn't be hanging out with people like that," I insisted.

"Girl, you ain't my mama. Nakiya's my girl; we been cool since fifth grade and she's always been there, so I would never drop her as a friend."

"Okay, well when you get raped or end up a witness in some kind of crime because of her friends and your association, don't say nothin'."

"Here you go again, always judgin'. Nakiya loves God just like you do, and God knows my heart. Just because I'm not ready to live like you don't mean that God loves me any less. You always telling other people how to live their lives, but you never look at your own. You treat yo' momma like crap, but that's not an issue to you. You so worried about me and my boyfriend that you can't even get along wit' yo own family, so don't tell me about hanging around people, 'cause maybe I shouldn't be around you." She stood up, looked at me, and walked away. I was in shock. I didn't know what I said was going to go that deep. I was still trying to figure out where I was wrong.

After about an hour I found Kristen in a bridal shop looking at dresses. She was still upset, but I could tell she had calmed down.

"Hey, did you find a dress?"

"Yeah, I found three actually, but I really like this one." The dress she showed me was black with spaghetti straps and had an extremely low back; the front was low, and on the sides were slits covered with a black sheer material. The dress fishtailed out with lace trim at the bottom. She tried it on and when she bent over, I saw way too much.

"It's okay, but don't you think it's kind of low?" I asked.

"Naw girl, it's just right."

I figured this was the perfect time to apologize for my tone. I have to remember to not be so judgmental sometimes. It's always a way to say things, and even if it was true; I could have said it in a different way.

"Hey Kristen, I want to say I'm sorry for the way that I spoke to you earlier."

I waited to see if she had anything to say, but her face was real stoic.

"You know my intention is always that you become everything that you are called to be, so when you tell me about situations like that, it makes me angry that you allow yourself to be around people who do those types of things."

Kristen walked into the dressing room and I followed her in. I was waiting to hear her response, but she seemed as if she wasn't hearing me.

"A.J, I know that what Nakiya is doing is wrong, but I have no control over her. All I can do is hope that she grows out of it. As for me, I do what I want to do. I appreciate the fact that you care, and that is why I'm not trippin', 'cause I know it's out of love, and I know you crazy." She cracked a smile and turned around to unzip her dress.

"Well, just know that I love you, and I want the best for you, and when you want the best for you, then you will understand my frustration." She rolled her eyes and smiled, and I hugged her.

"Love ya cuz."

Now, I started trying on dresses, starting with a light blue tube top dress with beads everywhere; it had a low back and a slanted cut at the bottom. After about twelve dresses and two hours, I found the dress I wanted. It was a cream strapless gown that had gold and cream beads running through to the bottom. The top had gold beads going across and the bottom fishtailed out.

"Girl, you look good!" When I came out of the dressing room, Kristen and my mom were out there looking like I just won Miss America. "Yeah, Sweetie, I like that one. You wanna get it?"

"Yeah, I like it. It's cute and it feels good on my skin." I started to think about how much James would like it. Man, I couldn't wait until Homecoming. It was really going to be a beautiful night.

CHAPTER 5

CALLED OUT

.J., what are you doing? I want to use the phone; can you hurry up?" Justin bit into his apple right in front of my face while I sat at the computer typing my paper and talking to James.

"You want to call me later, Sweetie?"James asked.

I rolled my eyes and pushed Justin in his face. "Naw, you straight; he can wait. He just wanna call his little girlfriend."

"Whatever, A.J., I'm sorry, but I like to talk to her, okay, and I would like to call her before the night is over, so can you hurry up?"

Justin was getting old. Already, he was in ninth grade with a girl-friend; who would have thought? It seems just like yesterday when he was tearing the heads off of my Barbies, and now he likes real girls. He was getting cute, too. He was almost 6 feet, and he looked like my dad but had the light brown complexion of my mother. I still wondered where he got those light brown eyes. I was gonna have to watch him around those little Private School girls he knew. He wanted to go to an all boys' school, so now his hormones were in overdrive.

His little girlfriend was a trip, too. She was thicker than me and looked like she could be in my grade. She came over one night to watch a movie with Justin in the basement. I was shocked my parents allowed it. Of course, my uncle Mike allowed everything, and he was with my uncle all the time, so God only knew what he had done over there. But for some strange reason, I knew he hadn't done anything too disappointing.

"James, I'll see you tomorrow in school."

"Alright Babe, you have a good night." We hung up and I pushed my brother. I forgot that even though he was younger than me, he was still stronger; he pushed my head back and grabbed the phone from my hand. I walked away making funny faces and went into my room.

By this time, James and I had been talking for about two weeks, Homecoming would be this Friday, and I was really excited. I couldn't wait for him to pick me up in that new pearl Jaguar S-type that his father bought his mom for her birthday. I was so excited. I just hoped that I wouldn't mess up by doing something with James that I wasn't supposed to. I needed God to give me strength because for the last couple of days, James and me had been close, sometimes too close.

This past Tuesday, I went back to his house after school because we had a half-day and I didn't feel like going home. We watched a movie and got half way through the movie before he started telling me how much he cared about me and how important I was in his life. His hand went from caressing my arm to rubbing my leg, and before I knew it he was on top of me and I was rubbing his back kissing him and holding him.

After about fifteen minutes, he jumped up. To tell you the truth, I wanted to continue, but he was the one that said that we should stop; we were getting too close. His hands felt so good on my body, just holding me and caressing me, and now that I think about it, he did a pretty good job considering the fact that he's still a virgin. At any rate, I told him I should just leave and that was that. It was so hard to leave, but I had to do what God needed me to do.

"Hey Kiva, I have a question for you." My brother peeked his head in the door.

"Wassup?" I said reading over my notes from school. I knew it was something serious because my brother never asks me anything, except to get off the phone.

"How do you know when you love someone?" I looked up in amazement. My little brother thought he loved his little girlfriend.

"Well, does it seem like you want to be a better person when you're with her?"

"Yes."

"Are you extra considerate to her needs when you're around her?"

"Sometimes."

"Do you think that you can see yourself with her for a long time?"

"Yeah ... I mean, at least until prom."

"Well, my little brother, you probably love her then." He sat there looking me in the face as I continued to look over my notes.

"What's the problem? I told you that you love her; call her and tell her or something.

"Well, there's a problem." He looked serious.

"What is it?"

"She's not saved."

"Dump her," I said, turning away. He scooted closer on the bed and reached for my shoulder.

"But how can you tell me to witness to others, to show an example and to love my neighbors, and then tell me to break up with my girlfriend?" I turned and looked at him as if he was stupid.

"Boy, you know that word just like I do, and it specifically says do not be unequally yoked with other people. Now if you want to be her friend and minister to her, fine, but don't think that your relationship is going to grow; you're always going to have problems if she doesn't agree with how you want to live. Believe me, I know, it doesn't work."

"Well, I mean I can change her. It's not like she doesn't believe in God at all, I can show her how to be a Christian."

I walked over to my vanity, threw my notes down, turned around, and looked at him again. "Justin, listen to me, she is not saved, and you cannot save her; only God can. All you can do is help." I fell on the bed and pulled a pillow under me. "I'm not telling you to break up with her, but you have to talk to God about it; you never know what God has up his sleeve. His ways are not our ways. Remember when I dated Mike? It was the same situation, you're going to get tired of trying to please her and still be true to your beliefs."

He looked down to the ground and started fidgeting with his finger-nails. I knew he had more to tell me.

"What else is on your mind?" He looked at me as if to say, "If you only knew."

"Well, Jessica and I have been together for about six months now, and we have been through a lot." Personally I don't understand how two 15-year-olds can go through a lot, but I continued to listen.

"Go ahead, tell big sis everything." I tried to hug him and he pulled away.

"Jessica and I chilled at uncle Mike's last weekend and we were watching a movie."

Oh Lord, here it comes. Me and my brother were close, but If he tells me what I think he's about to tell me, I don't know what I'm going to do.

"Yeah, how was the movie," I asked casually.

"It was cool." He chuckled and looked out the door to see if Mom or Dad were coming.

"Anyway, uncle Mike left, so we were still there, and we started kissing and stuff, you know how that goes. Anyway, she was feeling so good, and I asked her if she wanted to stop, and she said no, so I continued. But to make a long story short, fifteen minutes later, she was putting her clothes back on and I was laying on the floor in shock."

"Justin!" I screamed and hit him in the head with my pillow. "You had sex with that girl!"

He pushed me down on the bed and put his finger over my mouth just in case our parents heard me.

"Kiva, you don't understand, it felt so good. I can't describe it!"

"So now what?" I asked.

"Well, my flesh wants more, but my spirit is hurting. I asked God for forgiveness. I mean Kiva, the sex was good, too good. But God knows how I felt after I came down from my shock, and if I gotta feel like that after every time, I don't know if I could stand it."

"But me and Jessica are going to work it out," he said, standing up and looking at himself in the mirror. I walked over to my rocking chair and sat down looking at how vain my brother was looking.

"Well, does she want to give it up? I mean, sounds like if she's not saved, this is just another part of the relationship for her."

"If I tell her that it's a conflict, then she'll chill out."

"Justin, she's gonna say, 'well if you thought it was a conflict, why did you have sex with me in the first place,' and then you're gonna look stupid. I know I can't tell you what to do, but you came in here for my advice and I think—"

"Akiva, it doesn't matter, all you're gonna say is break up with her, and I'm not feelin' that. I love her, and whatever I need to do to keep her, I will."

I couldn't believe my little brother was standing up for his little girlfriend. What can I say, I didn't want to turn him away by telling him that he needed to dump her, but I didn't want to give him the impression that it was okay to have sex and still think that he was still living the life.

"Well, Justin, I mean honestly, you gonna have to go to God, because I'm not gonna sugar coat anything, and you not gonna get mad at me because I'm telling you how to live your life, but just remember, you are accountable for you." He looked at me with a blank face and as soon as he was about to speak, the phone rang.

"Oh, it's probably Jessica. Alright sis, I'll holla." He walked out of my room, and I got up and turned on the TV. Two minutes later, he peeked his head in the door.

"Oh yeah, and Kiva." I looked up from the TV.

"Yes?"

"Good looking out." He smiled and ran down the stairs.

CHAPTER 6

H ello, may I speak to Ananda?" I got back in my rocking chair and pulled a cover over my legs to keep warm.

"This is she. Hey Kiva, what's goin' on?" Ananda was the closest friend I had in the world. Monique and I were close friends, but Ananda and I were like sisters. She lived in Ann Arbor, so I only saw her at church and sometimes when we decided to go somewhere. We had known each other since middle school and understood each other, but we also knew that we couldn't be around each other for long periods of time because we just had different ways of doing things. I would say, we had a quota, so to speak.

"Hey girl, I was just seeing how you were doing." She could tell by the tone of my voice that it was so much more to it.

"Kiva, I guess you thought you were talking to someone that doesn't know you like the back of my hand; what's going on?" I started pacing the floor and trying to figure out how to tell her my feelings without sounding like a heathen.

"Well Ananda, you know I've been talking to James for about two weeks, and you know I've practically been in love with him since freshman year."

"Yes, I know this information."

"Well, I mean, Homecoming is coming up, and I am trippin', I just don't—"

"Let me stop you there. Are you trying to imply that you have been saving yourself for seventeen years and you are willing to give it up all because you think, and I don't use the word think lightly, that he is 'the one'? Who have you been hanging around, because you not making any sense." I sat back on my bed and started to think about what she said. She was right, but it didn't make a difference; I still wanted to get some.

"I mean, I haven't been hanging around anybody out of the usual."

"Oh, so it's Kristen. You need to watch her, girl. I know that's blood, but you keep on acting like this and that's goon' be you' hanging' buddy soon." Ananda couldn't stand Kristen. I guess she couldn't understand how a fifteen-year-old could just be out there like Kristen was. I admit that Kristen was bad, but I try not to make a habit of judging people, plus I knew Kristen was gonna come around soon; I could feel it.

"That's my blood. I think I can show her some things, plus you don't know her like I know her." Every time we got on the phone, she talked about how Kristen needed to get her life together and how Kristen was embarrassing herself. Ananda really seemed concerned or just really didn't like her, and I wish I knew why.

"But Ananda, back to me, I mean James is so fine, we are going to be together anyway; why can't I just give myself to him?" I really didn't believe that, but I wanted to think it for a moment and try to justify it.

"Girl, please, how would he look at you if you talk about how saved you are and how close your relationship to God is with him, and then you turn around and give it up after three weeks? Most importantly, you gave God your word that your virginity was something that you were saving for your husband. I know it's hard to be patient, but just hang in there, you know his strength is made perfect in your weakness; he'll see you through."

I felt encouraged, but I still wanted some. So I decided to change the subject.

"Well, how are you and Jeffrey doing?" I inquired about her boyfriend of two years. He was saved, she was saved, and from the looks of it, they were actually going to end up together. Jeff went to her high school and after graduation planned to go to the University of Michigan. He told Ananda that he wanted to get engaged, so when they graduated they could get married.

"Girl, we're fine. We were talking about what schools we wanted to attend." I pulled my cover up to my neck and tried to sound happy for her.

"Well, if you're getting married anyway, does it matter?"

"We still want to be close. We both go to the same church, and we plan to get married there, so we kind of want to stay in the area." Ananda and Jeffrey made a cute couple. He was very fair skinned and tall, while Ananda was about 5'2 and had light brown skin. She had shoulder-length jet-black hair that she kept down all the time, and almond-shaped chestnut-colored eyes. She was very shapely and loved to wear skirts all the time. When we went out, people always thought we were twins because of our body shapes and complexions.

Jeff was a pretty boy. He had this real curly hair that he wore at the top of his head, and he wore these Versace glasses all the time. He was really cute, and whatever Ananda went through to keep him, it was well worth it. He treated her like a queen and always tried to respect her. He used to be a thug, and he still had some of that in him, but Ananda liked that, so I think that's what initially attracted her to him. I'm still trying to figure out how he was a thug but lived in Ann Arbor; maybe I just think too much.

"Kiva, understand that God is going to send you your perfect mate, and you just have to wait it out. Believe me, the hard part is when you get that perfect mate and you have to hold out for him. You start to think why, if he's the one, why can't we just go ahead, but you don't want to ruin anything, and being obedient to what God tells you is the most important. Seek him about strength for this time; girl, it's hard for me. Sometimes me and Jeff don't even see each other for days because we'll pounce on each other, but I know it'll be worth the wait."

"Well, how will I know if we're compatible if we don't have sex before?"

"If you feel that way, then you don't trust God to bring you that one person who can please you just how you want to be pleased. God created you, so he knows what you want. Just wait and pray. I know that sounds corny, but if you want to keep in his will, you goon' have to, that's the only way."

"You right girl; I don't know why I'm trippin'."

"I understand, believe me. I mean it's been nights when Jeff and I have stayed on the phone telling each other how we wish we could show each other how much we loved each other and how much we just wanted to please each other, but we couldn't, and it's all because of our love for God. You have to understand that God will honor that. He knows how we feel, and him knowing that we're still holding on is something that he is proud of."

I sat on the other end of that phone so much more encouraged. God knew. He knew all of my thoughts, dreams, goals and aspirations. I knew calling her would help. When I first met Ananda, I didn't like her, and now when I look back on how far we have come in our relationship, I knew that she was sent from God. I remember six months ago having this same conversation with her, and encouraging her not to let go of the promise that she made with God. I look at the seed I sowed and how it came back to me one hundred fold. God is faithful and true. I mean, why would I ever want to disappoint the true lover of my soul?

"Girl, you right. I don't know what I was thinking."

"I'm glad you called me, girl, 'cause I was bored anyway. You wanna do something?" It was Sunday night and I knew my mom wasn't gonna let me drive 45 minutes away to go visit Ananda.

"You wanna meet at the movies at about 8:30?" It was a long drive for either of us, but if we came in different cars, then we could be on our separate ways at the end of the night.

"That's cool, I'll ask my mom and call you back in a few minutes." I hung up and searched the house for my dad. I knew what my mom was going to say, but looking at the situation, it seemed like I didn't have a choice.

"Mom, where's Dad?" I asked, walking into the kitchen. My mom was in the process of cooking a whole chicken and listening to one of her old gospel CDs. The smells of chicken, Mama's special green beans, and cornbread filled the air.

"Oh Sweetie, he had to go up to the church for a staff meeting. What's up?" My mom was a happy woman. She loved to cook, read, take care of her children, and praise God. I just didn't understand where the happiness came from, and sometimes I wondered if it was fake.

"Um, I just wanted to know could I go to the movies with Ananda tonight? You know we hardly get to see each other, and I should be back by 10:00 or 10:30." I leaned on the kitchen counter and grabbed an apple from the fruit bowl. My mom turned off the oven and pulled the chicken out, put the hot pads on the table, wiped her forehead, and looked at me as if she had a thousand other tasks to do.

"Sweetie, you know tomorrow you have school. I have to call your dad and make sure it's okay." Here we go. Why couldn't she be the woman of the house and just say yes. Nothing ever went out of this house without it going through Reginald first.

"Mom, the movie starts at 8:30 and it's 7:30 now, by the time you get in touch with him it's gonna be after 8, can't you just make—" It was too late; she had already picked up the phone and dialed the church number.

I rolled my eyes and sat in the nook with the green beans. While the phone was ringing, she walked over to the refrigerator and pulled out some juice for me to drink.

"Hello, may I speak to Deacon Niran, please? Hey Sweetie, um Kiva wants to know can she and Ananda go to the movies tonight? It's okay?"

Before she got off the phone, I was already up the stairs. I blasted some music and looked through my closet for an outfit. Finally I found the perfect jeans and shirt to wear. I sat in front of my mirror and tried to decide what make-up to wear. My skin is caramel brown and my eyes are oval shaped, so I always use a lot of eye shadow. Since I needed my hair done, I decided to throw my hair into a ponytail and put some cute earrings on. By the time I was fully dressed, it was 8:10 and I had to hurry to the theatre. I grabbed my purse and cell phone and ran down the stairs.

"Kiva, Ananda called after you ran upstairs; she said she would meet you up there."

I had forgotten all about that. When I get so riled up about how I want stuff to run, I forget the whole purpose.

✞✞✞✞✞

I pulled up in the movie theatre parking lot in my mom's Taurus looking for a four-door dark green truck with a license plate that said "dwn2erth," which happened to be the exact opposite of Ananda's mother. Latanya Bracha was a smart woman who married the right man at the right time, just when he became rich. She didn't work, cook, clean, or anything that didn't involve shopping. Don't get me wrong, she's a nice lady, but high maintenance.

Ananda surprisingly didn't take after her in those traits. Ananda could sing, and she loved to be in the spotlight, but as far as everything else, she was pretty down to earth. I found a parking spot in the back of the theatre and called her from my car. "Girl, where you at? It's 8:35 and the movie already started." I pulled down my mirror to check my make up and hair.

"I'm in the movie theatre with the tickets, waiting for you."

"Oh, okay. Bye."

I walked in the movie theatre and spotted her right off. Ananda had on a honey- colored off-the-shoulder sweater that kind of showed her stomach, some low rider jeans that had the same color stitching near the bottom of the pant, and some matching boots that were to die for. Her hair was a tad bit longer than mine, and she had put light brown highlights in it. She had a Louis Vuitton shoulder bag, two tickets in one hand, and a big bag of popcorn in the other.

"Hey, Girlie, I missed you." She smiled and gave me a hug.

"Yeah, I see you wasn't at church today; apparently you went shopping." She stepped back and turned around to show me her new outfit.

"Girl please, I went to my cousin's church today, and after that I went shopping. You like?"

"Very cute." I commented, as she strutted her stuff back and forth like she was on a runway. That was the big difference between us. We were both short and the same complexion, but unlike her, I embraced my shortness. Timberlands, Nikes, and S. Carters were my preferred style, while Miss Ananda preferred Nine West, stilettos and spiked heels.

We found seats and watched the movie, but within an hour, I was ready to go. I knew we shouldn't have gone to the Platinum Theatre, but I was trying to be accommodating. The movie was already ghetto, and on top of that, everybody either was on the phone, trying to talk to folks, or just being loud.

"Hey Boo, how you like the movie?" A voice behind me asked. I wanted to say that I really didn't know because you and your boys had been talkin' the whole time, but I decided to be nice.

"It's fine, thanks." Ananda laughed at my dry reply and slid down in her seat to avoid any conversation.

"Well, I mean, why you come wit' yo girl? Why you didn't have yo man bring you?"

Why was he still talking to me? By this time I had given up all hope of finishing the movie, so I decided to humor him. I turned around to the cutest guy I had ever seen. I couldn't even speak.

"Well, um, uh he's at home? Where's your girl at?"

"Well, I thought I found her, but she seems to have a man; why you ain't wait for me?" He licked his lips and sat up in his chair. He had on a big black jacket with fur around the hood. His jacket was halfway open so I could see his black and grey sweater and his chain. I caught a whiff of his cologne and I had to pull Ananda out of her seat.

"I mean, what you got that my man can't give me?" I inquired.

"Well, whateva you want Boo, I got it; just ask." He pulled out a wad of money wrapped in a rubberband. He stuffed it back in his pocket while grazing the top of his cell phone.

"How about we end this conversation right now?" I suggested, hoping that God would come down and rescue me before I got myself in any trouble.

"Alright then, Sweetie."

An hour later, the lights went up. We sauntered out into the hallway and ran smack dab into my mystery man.

"It's good to see you in the light," he declared, looking me up and down.

"Yeah, you too," I said, looking at those thick lips and that flawless skin. He turned his head to the side and the earring almost hurt my eyes. He was starting to be a little questionable.

"So what's yo name, Baby?"

"Akiva. What's yours?"

"Alex. That's a pretty name, Kiva." He came closer to me and grabbed my hand.

"So you think I can get your number or something? I'm a gentlemen, I could show you a real good time."

I bet he could, with his fine self. I had to pull myself together. "I told you I had a man." He put his hand to his mouth, chuckled and showed his pretty white teeth to me.

"Kiva, you're a sweet girl. You turned around and inquired what could I do for you, and I'm trying to show you. What's the harm in a little putt-putt golf?"

He was kinda right, and I mean James and I weren't officially boyfriend/girlfriend, so it was technically okay.

"Alright, I'll give you my cell phone number," I said reluctantly. We exchanged numbers, and walked away. I couldn't believe it. But hey, it was done. I found Ananda sitting on a bench on her phone, so I pulled her to come on. Right when I was about to walk out the door, I heard Alex call a name.

"O, come on man, let's go!" I looked over to my right in the crowded theatre and saw Oliver, Kristen's boyfriend, hugged up on some other girl.

My mouth dropped. Alex walked over and pulled Oliver's arm while he kissed the girl on her neck and put his hand to his ear in a phone like position. I couldn't believe it.

"Ananda, let's go." I said, pulling her arm.

"Why are we rushing?" She almost tripped over her shoes.

"I'll tell you when we get outside."

"Alright."

CHAPTER 7

No, I can't believe it. I wish I was there!" Monique said at lunch. I figured I had to tell somebody, and I was still debating whether I was going to tell Kristen or not.

"Girl, Alex was fine, okay, and he had bank, mad bank. But I still want James, you know?"

She looked at me as if I was crazy. "Girl, you betta get with the program. He offering to take you out, buy you nice things, you betta get it while the gettins' good!" All I could do was shake my head.

"So are you gonna tell Kristen? I mean, that's your cousin."

I wasn't sure yet. "I mean, she would hate me for it, and then she would believe his word over mine anyway, and besides, why interfere in her relationship? Knowing her, she already knows." Monique looked at me in disbelief and continued to eat her food.

"Oh, here comes boo #1." I hit her arm as James walked up to our table.

"Hey Kiva, I missed you last night. Your mom said you went out." He put his books on the table and scooted close to me.

"Well, I'm about to go to my locker before I go to class, so I'll see you Kiva. Bye, James." Monique walked off and it was just us three at the table—me, James, and my guilt.

"Yeah, I went to the movies with Ananda, one of my girlfriends."

"That's cool. Look, uh, Kiva we need to talk."

What now? I was already on edge.

"Wassup?"

"Well, I want to apologize for some of my behavior the last couple of weeks. I have been really out of myself. I mean, Kiva, you don't understand how it feels to finally chill with someone on my level, and especially for it to be you, you know. I need to be more of a gentleman with you and that I can't expect for us to get past the physical factor if we keep putting ourselves in that position, so I really just wanted to apologize."

Great. Just great. When I wanna be a rebel, that's when God shows me how stupid I was for doing it. Who was I kidding? I've wanted James for a long time, and now that I had him, I didn't want to lose him, especially not over a guy who ain't about nothing.

He grabbed my chin and looked at me with his light brown eyes. "Kiva, I want to start over, the right way. I want to date you for you and not your body. If we can't spend time at each other's houses watching movies, then so be it. But that's what I want, if it's okay with you?" He let go of my chin, twisted his baseball cap to the side, and waited for my reply.

"Yeah, I want that. I know if we start over we can make this work." I smiled and shrugged my shoulders. He stood up and grabbed my books with a big grin on his face.

"Can I walk you to class?"

"Please do; I want you to."

✝✝✝✝✝

"Kiva, don't throw your book bag right there. Take it upstairs." She was always cleaning up! Talk about a neat freak.

"Yes, Mom."

"And go get ready for dinner. It should be done in about fifteen minutes." I could smell the catfish, green beans, mashed potatoes, and baby carrots already. If my mom knew how to do anything, it sure was cook.

I moseyed into the kitchen and sat on one of the stools by the counter. As I watched my mom cut up some lemons and put them in the Kool-Aid for dinner, I realized how much my mom worked for this family and never got recognized. Come to think of it, I never even remember thanking her for making dinner, not one time. She wiped off the counter where she was cooking and looked up to see me staring at her.

"Sweetie, is there something you want to ask me?" I sat there wondering a lot of things, but not actually wanting to speak them.

"No, I just wanted to know what time was Daddy coming home." I watched her face drop from excitement at the thought of us actually bonding for a minute to the silent frustration of knowing that her only daughter is closer to her father than to her.

"He should be home any minute now. He had to pick Justin up from baseball practice."

"Mom, how did you and Dad meet?" I put my elbow on the counter and leaned toward her. She looked surprised and her face lit up.

"Well, your father and I met in college. We were both in the same campus ministry, but your dad was one of those guys who came but wasn't really active. After awhile, we started to date, and I knew he was the one."

"But why did you date him if he wasn't active?" I couldn't see a time where my father wasn't praising the Lord somewhere or somehow.

"Well, we didn't start dating until he actually got his life together, but I had a crush on him for a long time. Then I graduated and your father was the president of the ministry; it was called G2 or God's Grace Ministries. After I moved to Baltimore for graduate school, we both got closer to God, and then we got back together. I got the job as an editor, and he found a job as an architect. God blessed us and showed us a valuable lesson."

"And what was that?" I was confused. They didn't go through any heartache or pain, so how did God show them anything?

"Well, we learned patience. He said that if I hadn't graduated and left the state, he probably wouldn't have become president of the ministry. That's also how he met our pastor. If I hadn't been obedient, then I probably would have tried to stay here with your father, and I wouldn't have all the experience I got over in Baltimore, which made me more than qualified to come back and get a position that usually people with 10 or 12 years of experience get. Since we learned to lean on Christ, we live in a wonderful house, with two beautiful children, not wanting for anything, and blessed coming in and going out. God blessed us because we listened, we took heed, and didn't put anything before him."

"Wow, patience, huh." I helped her set the table and decided to ask her more questions about her college days.

"So, did you have sex before you were married?" I knew that would catch her off guard. She stopped in her tracks and looked at me as if I was crazy. "I mean, Mom, I feel like I should know these things."

"And why is that?" she inquired while walking into the kitchen to get the rest of the food.

"Well, Mom, you are someone I come to for comfort and knowledge. If I know the mistakes you made, maybe I can learn from them and make better decisions."

"Oh, you're gonna make the better decision," she said, bringing out the bowl of baby carrots.

"Oh, so you did, huh!" I fell into one of the dining room chairs and looked at my mom in shock. "Does dad know?"

"Sweetie, I never said yes or no."

"But mom, I want to know." I grabbed her arm in pseudo desperation.

She looked at me for a moment, like she was deciding how much to tell me.

"Well, I will tell you this, when I was your age, I spent a lot of time with my girlfriends. We would go to the mall, movies, and different things like that you know."

I was nodding my head on the outside and wondering where this was going on the inside.

"When I started to date boys, my father was very protective. I had an early curfew and I really wouldn't even call it dating because guys knew my father was no joke. I never understood why your grandfather was so protective, it seemed to me that he treated my mom with so much love and respect, bought her nice things, and took her places, why wouldn't he want that for me?"

I was still waiting for her to bring it on home.

"But once I got to college, I started to see how much my friends went through. I was so shy from not really dating in high school, but my girl-friends in college were pros! They knew all the cute guys' names, knew where they stayed, where they hung out and all that. After so many years of them chasing after these guys, I saw the constant heartbreak from the boys cheating on them, I saw the pregnancies that pulled bright girls out of school, and I heard about the diseases that were given with no warning. By the end of my sophomore year, I knew that I wasn't going to settle for some guy who claimed they were gonna sweep me off my feet, buy me things and take me places, because if they did, it was all just to get one thing, and they couldn't have that, girl. It's too precious."

She made a whole lot of sense.

"So, Mom, guys were really doin' your friends wrong? How could a man be that mean to a woman?"

She smiled and walked over to my side of the island.

"Baby, boys treat women like that, not men. Your father is a man, your brother is growing up to be a man. One day, you will marry a man."

We both laughed.

"Kiva, one thing you have to understand about these boys out here, is that a lot of them know how to talk a good game. They know how to make you feel all good and tell you all the right things, but when it comes time for their actions to line up with their words, they won't do it. The reason why, varies, but usually it's selfishness."

That made so much more sense. She was schooling me right now.

"That's so crazy man, I'm glad that I haven't put myself in that type of situation."

"Kiva, you know I didn't have the opportunities that you've had to learn about what God has for you, and how to get pleasure out of seeking God first above all things. But God sent me you to let you learn from my mistakes and mold you into a better person than I was at your age. Don't let the pleasures of the flesh get to you. They only last a few minutes and they're never satisfying. God is the ultimate satisfier and the lover of your soul. With him, you will never lack. He will never stand you up for a date, mistreat you, do you wrong, or leave you. That is who you learn from when you get found by your mate, if he has those God-like qualities, then pray about it. God will move and open your eyes to things you would have never seen about that person. Just trust."

I was intrigued by every word she said; this was the most we had ever talked in my whole life. To my surprise, I enjoyed it. Five minutes later, the door opened and my father and brother came in.

"Hello Ladies, how y'all doin'?" Dad gave me a hug and kissed my mom on the cheek.

I turned to Justin. "Hey punk, how was school?" He looked at me, smirked, and shoved me in the back.

"It was great, how was it for you?"

"Ouch, Justin; you suck."

He pushed me down into the chair and went upstairs to clean up for dinner. I began to help Dad set up the dinner table, and we all set down, as a family.

CHAPTER 8

CALLED OUT

"ey Lady, how was your day?" James called at ten o'clock, and I was in the basement watching TV.

"I'm cool, just tired." I slouched more into the couch.

"Are you excited about Friday?"

"Yes, I can't wait actually." I thought about Homecoming and how pretty I was going to look, and how fine James was going to be, I decided that I was going to get my hair spiral curled all over with some light brown highlights.

"I miss you, James. I hardly got to see you all day today," I said with childlike sadness in my voice.

"I miss you too, Boo. You know basketball season is about to start, so I have to start training with coach and stuff, but don't worry, Im'ma have you all to myself on Homecoming night."

I smiled and laid down on the couch. We had been doing so well this past week; we hadn't kissed or been all up on each other. Monique asked me were we still together because we walked down the hallway without his arm around my waist, and I hadn't been talking about him much lately. I was just tryin' to chill with her without bringing him into the conversation, and besides, we still didn't go together yet. Five minutes later, my cell phone rang.

"Hold on, James." I didn't recognize the number but decided to answer it anyway.

"Alright."

"Hello," A deep voice sent chills down my spine.

"Hello, may I speak to Kiva?"

"Yes, who is this?"

He laughed and then paused. "You don't remember me? It's Alex, Boo; wassup wit chu'?"

I was shocked. It had been three days since I gave him my number, and so much had gone on in my life since then, I forgot that he was supposed to call. He sounded so good, but did I want to talk to him?

"Hey Alex, hold on, okay?" I put my cell phone down and picked up the house phone.

"James, I'm gonna call you back, okay?" I felt bad, but he didn't know what I was about to do, and it wasn't like I was cheating.

"Alright, call me before you go to bed, okay?"

"Alright," I said nervously. I reached for the cell phone, wondering what this boy had to say.

"How you been?"

He was so laid back, I could just picture him sitting in a chair, slouching down, with his head back.

"Nothin', just chillin'." I tried to sound just as cool as he did.

"Was you on the phone? You could have called me back."

"I mean I was on the phone, but you cool." We talked for about an hour. I found out he was a 21-year-old commuter student to Oakland University.

"You should come visit me when I move on campus. You know we can chill or whateva."

"That would be cool. What high school did you go to?"

"I went to Wayne High, but my cousin goes to your school, Shawndra Moore. You know her?" I almost jumped out of my seat.

"Do they call her Shawny?" I was hoping it wasn't who I thought it was.

"Yeah, she in your grade too; she light-skinned and tall." I could have screamed. Why oh why oh why did he have to be related to the one girl who liked James! My life was just not getting any better, what could possibly happen next?

"Yeah, I know her; she cool." I said dryly. "Do you talk to her a lot?" I asked, hoping the answer would be no.

"Naw, I mean we related, but she be on some other stuff. But let's talk about me and you, and when I can see you again."

I knew it was wrong, but he was so cool. One date couldn't hurt right?

"I mean, when you wanna see me?"

"What about this weekend?"

"I can't." He didn't have to know about Homecoming.

"Alright, well what about Thursday? Do your parents let you go out during the week?"

"Just as long as I'm back by 10:30."

"Cool, well what if I pick you up from school and we chill until you ready to go home?" I looked at the phone and wondered was he crazy. What were we gonna do from three until ten o'clock at night?

"How about you pick me up from my house around five and we can figure out what we're gonna do then."

"That's cool. Alright, Sweetheart, I'm bout to go get something to eat, so give me a call tomorrow, alright?"

"Alright then."

I hung up the phone and realized that I just made a date with another guy the day before I was supposed to go out with James. I didn't want to tell him no, and I thought he was so cool. This was so staying a secret. I was so not telling Monique about this.

✝✝✝✝✝

I was so tired in first hour. I laid my head on my desk and tried to keep my eyes open while all the rest of the students chatted among themselves. It was really cold that morning, so I wore my cream and black turtleneck with my black jeans and my black and white boots. I had my black book bag on my back, and decided to pull my hair in a ponytail with a cute bang that morning. All in all, I was cute but tired. I asked the teacher if I could go to the bathroom and then walked into the hallway.

As I passed the green and white lockers and turned the corner to go up the stairs, the hallway began to smell like perfume and feet. I went into the bathroom and looked in the mirror to make sure my hair was still cute. I smelled smoke, but I didn't know where it was coming from; then Kristen came out of a stall.

"Kristen, what are you doing and why?" I asked, looking confused.

"O showed me how; he said I look sexy when I smoke, especially after we … never mind; you wouldn't understand." I dug in my purse to get my lip-gloss out and tried not to think about last Sunday.

"Oh yeah, he told me he saw you Sunday at the movie theatre." I looked at her in surprise. I tried to play it off as if I didn't see him, but she was up to my game.

"Yeah, I thought that was him, but I wasn't sure."

"Mmhmm, yeah, right trick. He told me that you and Alex exchanged phone numbers. Guess you want a rough neck, huh?" She laughed, threw her cigarette down, and smashed it into the green tile on the floor.

"He's cute, but that don't mean Im'ma talk to him."

"Girl please, he can wipe the floor with James. All James got is those dimples."

I was trying to think of something to say without saying anything at all.

"Girl whatever, he was cute, he's a bad boy though, so ain't nothing gon' happen with us."

"So why did you give him your number then, Kiva? Huh, he so bad for you, he got a one-way ticket to hell, and I know you ain't trying to minister to him. Give me and yourself a break today, okay?" She walked out of the bathroom and didn't look back. She was right, I needed to get my priorities straight, but she didn't need to know that. It is a process.

James gave me a ride home, and I felt so bad about what had happened the night before that it made me sick.

"Baby, are you okay? You don't look too good."

"Yeah, I'm straight. Can you just take me home?" I asked innocently.

"Okay. I hope you feel better on Friday, 'cause I wanna see you in that dress you been talking about." I looked at him shyly and smiled. He was so good to me, even when I wasn't any good to him. I hoped this wouldn't catch up to me. I got out of the car, waved to him, and continued to slowly stroll up the walkway to my house. Before I could even turn the knob, my cell phone rang.

"Hello."

"Wassup, Shortie? It's me, Alex." Why was I not surprised? His voice sounded so good on the phone.

"Nothing much." Suddenly the knots in my stomach loosened.

"So what time you want me to scoop you?"

"You can come at seven. I have dance class in thirty minutes." Thank God for dance class, although it just made me anxious to see him after class.

"Alright then, I'll call you at seven."

"Alright." I threw the phone on the couch in a mix of disgust and excitement. I didn't understand why I was doing this. He was fine, but he wasn't worth losing James over. I ran upstairs and fell on my bed trying to think of something we could do or somewhere we could go without being noticed, and without him trying to feel up on me. I looked at the clock and realized I only had ten minutes to get to dance class, so I grabbed my dance bag, a bottle of water, and a small towel, and I was off.

✝✝✝✝✝

"And up, and turn and kick and slide, step, leap, step leap, turn and pose." Mrs. Pilsner and her ballet drills were the last thing on my mind. As I glided across the floor, I started to think about how God works. When God uses his people to do things, he assigns one person the job, but if that person doesn't do it, God creates another to do the job. Even though it may sound like I'm making excuses for myself, maybe I could minister to Alex. I mean, as long as I don't get too close.

"Alright, class, I want to see everybody front and center to do *releve's*. And up, and up, and up, and, up ..."

My mom picked me up from dance class and as she drove, I slouched in the seat. Riding down Greenfield, I got nervous. I was excited about my date with Alex but still nervous. I wanted to show the world that I could make a positive difference in this man's life, and that by the time I was finished with him, he wouldn't even know what hit him. I got out of the car and grabbed my bag, relieved that this day was almost over.

"Hey Sweetie Pie, how was class?" My father was in the kitchen cutting up an apple and watching ESPN. My father loved sports with all his heart. If I could rate the things in his life that meant the most, one would be God, two would be mom/sports, three would be sports, sports again, and finally his beloved children, but me first, of course.

"Daddy, it was straight. Um, I have a date tonight." I hoped he would tell me no.

"With who?" he inquired while chopping the apple in fourths with a big knife.

"Well, Dad, I met him at the movies, and his name is Alex. He hangs out with Kristen's boyfriend." I threw out all the wrong information, hoping he would put his foot down like he usually does.

"Okay, so wait, Alex hangs out with Kristen's boyfriend, the cousin you don't care for that much, and you met him at the movies. Is he in school?

"Yes, he goes to Oakland."

"Community?"

"No, Daddy, University." I knew what the next question would be.

"Is he saved?"

"Well, Daddy, he … uh …"

"Uh, no; you're not going."

"But Dad, he is trying to learn about God. I know the situation seems bad, but in the end, God will get the glory. He wants to know God for himself, but he didn't have the luxury to live in a house full of God-fearing people. I might be the only Bible he ever sees. Now do you want to risk that chance?" My dad walked out of the room as if I wasn't even talking.

"Okay Dad, I mean, if I can't go, then fine." I chided, hoping that this would be the end of the conversation.

"Kiva, I want you to go." I turned around in shock.

"Why, I mean, Dad, are you sure? It is a school night."

"No, I want you to see how the real world is. Bring the boy in so I can see what he looks like. You might be right, if he needs to meet some God-fearing people, you bringin' him to the right household." He sat back in his lazy boy chair and continued to watch TV. Dang, it didn't work; now I guess I had to go.

CHAPTER 9

Before I could even go upstairs, my cell phone rang.

"Hello."

"Hey, it's me. I'll be on my way in about fifteen minutes."

"Alright."

"One."

Wow, that was the fastest conversation I had ever had. I went to my room and tried to find something to wear. I picked out this red and black shirt with some black jeans and a red belt. I decided to wear my black gymshoes and my red and black book bag purse. I wanted to be cute, but not all the way. As I was finishing my make-up and walking back to my room, I heard loud bass from a car outside. I couldn't recognize the song because the bass was so loud. At that moment, I knew it was going to be a long night. I walked down the stairs expecting the bass to be much louder by the time he got in front of the door.

As I walked into the library to wait for him, the doorbell rang. My stomach was flipping upside down. I walked to the door, straightened my clothes, fixed up my hair as much as possible, and opened the door.

"Hey Kiva, how are you?" I could not believe my eyes. The look on my face could only tell you how surprised I was to see what was standing at my door.

He sauntered his way into the foyer. "These are for you." He handed me a half dozen roses with a card that said, "Just thinking of you."

"Thank you so much. You can have a seat in the library if you want." I went to go put the flowers in water. As I walked to the kitchen, I wondered what the devil was trying to cook up now. When I came back to the library, my dad was preaching to him about being a man and living up to God's standards.

"You see, as a young man, you have to be about God's business and his plan for your life. God has put something in all of us to complete for his glory, and that's something that you need to find out, son. It's pertinent to your future."

"Dad, what are you guys talking about?" I walked slowly into the library.

"Sports, Sweetie." I looked at Alex to see his expression; surprisingly, he looked interested.

"Well, you two have a good time. I'll see you by 10:00." He pointed at me and gave me a hug. "Alright, Daddy, I'll see you."

"Bye, Mr. Niran. You have a good evening, sir." We walked out of the door and to his car. He helped me into the seat of his Explorer and closed the door behind me. He looked so good in his outfit. He had on Khaki pants with a white and khaki colored button-up shirt, a leather pleated jacket with fur around the hood, and his famous Versace glasses. He had curly hair, and when I looked closely I could see that his eyes changed color. I wanted to fall out right then and there.

"So where are we going?" I asked.

"Oh, I gotta stop by my boys' house first and then we gonna go grab something to eat."

He turned the music up all the way, and I just thought about how cute we looked together. As we drove down the highway, I imagined us ten years from now, driving back to see my mom and my dad. I even saw our kids in the backseat. I turned around to look back there, but my dream was killed by a bunch of XXL magazines and a basketball. At any rate, I still saw him at least picking me up from school and everybody standing outside wondering, "Who is that picking up A.J.?"

We turned down a street with a row of beautiful houses, all with gardens and beautiful landscaping. We pulled into a driveway and saw four or five cars with the same logo on the back windows: "Dream Team." I had heard about car clubs, but I never knew anyone in them.

We got out of the car and walked to the backdoor. A dark-skinned guy with a piece of pizza in his hand came to the door and grabbed Alex's hand.

"Wassup, Alex, how you doin'?" His voice was light yet manly, and he seemed nice.

"Wassup, Rob? Man, this is A.J." Alex let me walk into the house first. We walked through the kitchen and into the living room. There were about fifteen people in the house, and all of them were either holding a drink or smoking something.

"Alex, how long are we going to be here?"

"Not long, Baby; just chill. My friends are home for break." I looked around and couldn't imagine these people being in college. I couldn't imagine going to school everyday and then still doing the things that people who don't have an education do to their bodies. It just didn't make any sense to me. I sat down on one of the couches while Alex went back into the kitchen to grab us something to drink. He brought me a Sunny Delight from the refrigerator and himself a bottle of water. I was surprised but happy it wasn't liquor.

"So you wanna play cards or something?" He scooted closer to me and put his arm around me.

"Naw, I just wanna chill and, you know, get to know you. I thought we were going to get something to eat" He looked at me and smiled. His teeth were so nice. He put his hand on my knee and scooted closer.

"How good you wanna get to know me?" He totally ignored my question about going out to eat.

I scooted back in surprise. "Not that well."

He laughed and moved his hand. "I can respect that. Well, you wanna go in the other room where it's quiet? We can watch TV."

"That's cool." I said reluctantly.

"Alright, I'll be right back." He got up and went over to talk to Rob. Two girls sat in Alex's seat. I wanted to tell them no, but the way that they were acting, I didn't even feel like dealing with the drama. One turned around and saw me sitting there.

"Hi," she said.

"Hello," I replied smiling at her unpleasing stare.

"Who are you?" She sounded upset that I was even on the premises.

"I'm Kiva. I came here with Alex."

She laughed a drunken laugh and turned back around. She then whispered to her friend, "I hope Lenise don't come by tonight." She turned back around and I could smell the sweet and sour smell of alcohol on her breath. "So, what school you go to?"

"I go to Community Tech."

"You still in high school? Dang, I thought you was older than that."
She chuckled.

"When did you graduate from high school?" I asked with an attitude.

"In 2 years ago."

"So you just graduated. You act like you graduated in '97 or something." She laughed and then looked at me seriously. "I know you here
with Alex and everything, but his ex-girl might come by, so be prepared."

"Be prepared for what? Alex ain't my man." I retorted.

She scooted closer to me, and I could smell the mix of her funk and
her perfume with the alcohol. "Girl, Lenise is crazy; she'll light this house
on fire. You don't wanna mess with her." I scooted away, hoping she was
done talking to me. Two minutes later, Alex came back and tugged my
jacket to follow him in the other room. He grabbed my hand, and we
walked up the wooden staircase, which led to a wide hallway that had
about five rooms, two on one side and three on the other. The one in the
middle was the bathroom.

We went into one of the rooms, and he shut the door behind us. The
room was light blue and had a big-screen television in the corner. There
was a black lazy boy chair, a dresser with a mirror, and a huge sofa. This
was a man's room.

"Do you wanna sit down?" He plopped onto the sofa.

"I'll be straight in the lazy boy." As I sat down, he laughed and called
me young under his breath.

I stood up and walked over to where he was sitting. "Look, I didn't ask
to come here, and just because I'm not as easy as those girls downstairs
maybe shows you how mature I really am. So you can call me young all
you want, but my mind is right on target, thank you."

"Girl, you know you sexy when you mad." He flashed those teeth at
me and that dimple, and I had no choice but to melt on the inside.

"Come here." He pulled me into his lap. "Girl, I know you got intel-
ligence; I knew that from when we first talked. You someone I could see
myself with, no drama, just chillin' and talking, you know. And if you
was my girl, I would take care of you; you wouldn't have to worry about
nothing. You seem down, and just by me bringing you around my boys
shows a lot."

I looked up at him and smiled.

"So now you wanna smile and be all up in my face, huh." He teased.

I laughed, and before I knew it, we were kissing. Our lips touched and I felt it all on the inside.

"Girl, your lips are so smooth," he whispered as he kissed my ear. I put my hand on his face and rubbed his smooth skin. He began to kiss my neck and I sat up in his lap for more comfort.

Just as it was about to get too heavy, Rob yelled up the stairs. "Dawg, Alex, man, come here for a second!" Alex told me to ignore it. Two minutes later Rob was banging on the door. "Dawg, open up for real man!"

Alex walked to the door and opened it. "Wassup?"

"Dawg, let me talk to you out here in the hallway." Five minutes later he came back in and told me to stay there until he got back. I really wanted to know what was going on; I was kind of scared. I started thinking about ways I could get home without getting in trouble and people I could call if something went down. For some strange reason, the only person I thought of was Kristen. Aunty Deborah was the only parent I knew who would let her child out of the house this late, 'cause I knew my mom and dad weren't havin' any of this. I knew this was a bad idea.

Alex came back in and told me that Rob thought his mom was home, so he was telling all the girls to leave and trying to clean up the place.

"So you about to take me home?" I inquired.

"Naw, we have to wait, 'cause Rob's girl is still here and you, so we just gon' wait."

I didn't understand the logic, but I had no choice. This is what I get. Rob came back up the stairs and told Alex to come back in the hallway. I turned on the TV and decided to watch it. He came back in and sat down like nothing happened.

"So, what's going on?"

"It's not his mom." Suddenly Rob guided his girlfriend into the room and grabbed Alex to come downstairs. I really didn't understand what was going on out there. Rob's girlfriend walked by me and said hi, and then flopped in the chair. She acted like this happened all the time.

"Excuse me, uh, do you know what's going on?" I asked politely.

"Yeah, Alex's ex-girlfriend is here and she is crazy, so he wants us to stay up here, 'cause girl, if she sees you, she's liable to cut you." I rolled my eyes in the back of my head and fell back on the couch. Me, of all people. Do I just attract drama or what?

I asked the girl her name. "Bianca," she answered. "What's yours?"

"My name is Akiva, but since you let me know what's going on, you can call me A.J."

She turned around in the chair and smiled. "I like that; it's creative. Where does the J come from?"

"My middle name is Jeslyn; it means wealth and beauty."

"Really," she replied. "What's your whole name?"

"Akiva Jeslyn Niran. It means protected and blessed with wealth and beauty eternal."

"Wow, that's sweet. Seems like your parents spent a lot of time thinkin' about that."

We talked a little more, but stopped when we heard a female voice downstairs.

"Alex, you my man, ain't you? You my man, right?"

"Lenise, baby, you broke up with me, why you trippin'?"

"Let's go upstairs and talk."

"No, why can't we stay down here?"

"I wanna go upstairs, in private."

"No, Lenise, stop. Don't be comin' up in Rob's house disrespectin' me and tryin' to run something that ain't yours. You said it was over two weeks ago, and I'm through; I ain't got time for it." Five seconds later, we heard footsteps coming up the stairs and Bianca and I got real nervous.

"Lenise, what did I say, huh?" Alex was yelling at her.

"What Alex? Why can't we talk upstairs in peace?"

Bianca pulled on my arm, and we both walked into the bathroom that connected two rooms. "I ain't tryin' to get cut up 'cause of him!" She whispered. We chuckled softly. I tried to think of how I got myself in this predicament anyway. Not being obedient and acting all boy crazy. This is what I get.

"Look, Lenise, go back downstairs. This ain't your house, go!"

"Baby," she said softly. "I'm tired of arguing. Why can't we go in the room and talk, okay?"

"Lenise, go downstairs; then we can talk." We heard feet going downstairs and we came back in the room. Finally they were all outside.

"You my man, ain't you Alex? I mean why you trippin'? You know we meant to be!"

"Lenise, what is you talkin about dude, this was all you!"

"Who is she Alex? I know you got somebody up there!"

By this time Bianca and I were looking out of the window trying not to be seen. Lenise was a Puerto Rican girl; where did he find one of those in Detroit? She could pass for black, though. You could tell she grew up around black people because of her speech and the way she was dressed. Her car was parked out front, blocking the driveway, and two girls were in the car. One was in the driver's seat, and the other was in the backseat yelling out the window. One was telling her to bust out his car windows, and the other was egging her on to smack him upside the head. Thank God I didn't have friends like that.

"Lenise, that ain't got nothing to do with you, okay? You doin' too much! All this drama I ain't tryin' to be wit you and yo crazy—"

She interrupted him by trying to slap him in the face. He shifted his head, and all I saw was his chain fly in the other direction. His boys grabbed her and pulled her back, and that's when her girls got out of the car.

"This is too much like a movie to me," Bianca commented.

"You ain't never lied," I replied. They all calmed down and walked back to the car.

"Keep all that away from here!" Rob yelled. "I ain't trying to go to jail 'cause of you." The boys all came back in the house and we came down-stairs. I was ready to go. All four of Alex's boys plopped back on the couch like nothing happened. Rob went to the kitchen, grabbed a beer from the fridge, and came back out.

"You wanna play cards?" Bianca inquired as we sat at the dining room table.

"Uh, no; I wanna go home."

"Well, Alex is in the kitchen; go talk to him." I got up from the table in disgust and anger and walked into the kitchen to find Alex on the phone telling somebody what happened. He had a beer in one hand.

"Alright, man, Im'ma call you back. Naw, I ain't dealing with that girl no more. She got too much drama in her life. Yeah man, I'll holla." He closed the phone, put it back on his hip, and held out his arm for me to come and hug him. "So, you ready to go get something to eat?"

CHAPTER 10

By the time I got home, I was too tired to think. I went up to my room, kicked off my shoes, fell on my bed, and cried. Then I began to pray. "God, how could I have been so far away from you tonight? Lord, I am so sorry for putting guys before you and for being stupid. I never meant to hurt you, and I hope that I can be a better child for your kingdom, Lord. Lord Jesus, take me back. I haven't focused on you in so long, and I am tired of the drama. You came here so that I wouldn't have to go through hurt, pain, shame, or defeat, and I believe it and receive your mercy and grace. Clean me, Lord; make me whole and love me like no one has ever loved me; be that true lover of my soul that you said you were." As soon as I finished praying, a Bible verse came to me: Jeremiah 29:11. I got up and grabbed my Bible from my dresser and flipped through the books until I found the verse. It read,

> *"For I know the plans I have for you," declares the Lord, "Plans to prosper you and not to harm you, plans to give you hope and a future. Then you will call upon me and come and pray to me, and I will listen to you. You will seek me and find me when you seek me with all your heart."*

I cried again. God loves me so much that instead of punishing me, he says that he has plans to prosper me and make me whole. What a mighty God I serve. Tonight, was the first night of the rest of my life. I was changing and doing everything to glorify God in my body. Just trying to fathom the love and mercy he has for me every morning was incredibly difficult, especially when I still can't forgive and forget. God forgives, forgets, and blesses in the midst.

Why would I want to serve any other god? My God is living, and I will forever trust in him and build my faith in him. For me, this was the night when I found out who God was for myself, not through Mama, Daddy, or Grandma. He showed me how he was my king and my savior, and I know he is the real and living God.

✝✝✝✝✝

"Today's the big day," Mom said on the way to school. It was only a half-day. After school, I would get my hair and nails done and my eyebrows arched. Then, I had an appointment to get my make-up done. I wouldn't be finished with my beauty transformation until about four, and Homecoming was at eight. So I had enough time to shower, eat, get dressed, and take pictures. God was good, and I was truly blessed.

I pulled my book bag out of the backseat and waved good-bye to Mom. As I walked into the school, I saw James talking to Kristen; when they saw me, she walked off and he came over. "Hi Sweetie, how are you?" He grabbed my book bag off my shoulder, gave me a hug, and walked me to my locker. His politeness made me nervous, but then I thought about it and realized that he was like this all the time.

"I'm good. The Lord and I had a long talk last night, and I rededicated my life to him."

He looked at me and smiled. "I'm glad, Kiva, but is there any reason that you felt you weren't doing right? I mean, you don't just rededicate for nothing." I looked down and opened my locker, trying to think of something to say. "Well, my life hasn't been as strong as it's supposed to be, and I have just been really distracted by a lot of things."

"Well, I'm glad you made the right decision, Kiva." He looked at the clock on the wall and gave me a hug.

"I gotta go Babe, I'll see you tonight." He smiled with those beautiful teeth."

Alright Baby, see you then." I was so excited for tonight!

Mom picked me up from school exactly at 11:15 and we were off to the beauty shop, but first we stopped to get something to eat. I hated hamburgers, so I got a salad and some fries.

"Nice combination," my mother said sarcastically.

"Thanks," I said grabbing my bag and pulling out a fry. "Mom, what were the qualities that you were looking for in a husband?" She smiled and turned to drive toward the salon.

"Honey, I needed to know that he heard from God, and that God was the head of his life."

"What do you mean 'hear from God'?"

"Right now, you being a single, Christian woman, and I mean single as in not married, your job is to concentrate on God and what he wants for your life, how he wants to use you and what you need to do to achieve that. When you get married, your husband is the head, which means you follow his lead. If your husband isn't led by the spirit, you won't be able to fully trust the decisions that he makes, because he's not following God; he's listening to himself, which is not wise."

"But if God made me, he made my thoughts, right?"

"True, Sweetie, but you also have to understand that his ways are not our ways. God may want you to go to school in Asia and save souls over there. You may not want that, but to do his will, you have to follow him and be obedient, then you'll see it was worth it to see all those people being blessed by God and knowing him, just because you listened. Baby, you are not here for yourself. You are here to preach the word of God and let people know he is risen and sitting at the right hand of the father. Isaiah 61 says that

> 'The spirit of the Lord God is upon me: because the Lord hath anointed me to preach good tidings unto the meek; he hath sent me to bind up the broken hearted, to proclaim liberty to the captives, and the opening of the prison to them that are bound.'

If that ain't telling me to go tell the world, then I don't know what is."

"Well, what if you don't know what you're supposed to do, or you think that you're not called to be a preacher?"

"The Bible says that he pre-destined us before the foundations of the earth, so I believe that everyone has a calling in life. You may not be called to preach; you may be an usher, a deacon, a lawyer, a teacher, a doctor, or even a singer. Whatever God put in you, when you start to walk in his will, you will find your ultimate purpose. Then and only then will it manifest and people will see the anointing on your life."

"Mom, how did we get on this subject?" We both laughed.

"Kiva, you have to know yourself before you give yourself to some-one else. If you don't know who you are in Christ and what is expected of you, it's hard to be in a relationship. It's like starting a new job with no understanding of what to do. You're going in blind, and that's how the enemy will try to sneak in."

"You're right, but I really like James, and he is saved, sanctified, and filled with the Holy Spirit."

"That may be true Sweetie, but are you sure you are supposed to be in a relationship with James right now? You went out on a date with someone else the other day, and a key to being in a relationship is trusting and being faithful to one another." I sat in silence, feeling embarrassed and slightly misunder-stood. She was right; either I would go on living like I wanted to, constantly staying in drama, or I was going to change and be better. It was my choice.

✝✝✝✝

"He'll be here in thirty minutes, Mom; hurry up!" I yelled as I zipped my dress on and waited for my mom to put on my jewelry. My whole family was downstairs, even Ananda, and I was not ready. I sat in that beauty shop from 12:30 until 3:00, so everything got pushed back an hour. I walked in the house at 7:30, rushing and trying to get my things together.

"Here I come, Baby." Mom rushed out of her bedroom with the jew-elry. In one hand she had a diamond-looking choker with matching earrings. She also had a real diamond tennis bracelet that matched the earrings and choker. The earrings were pear shaped and sparkled in the light. "Don't let your father know I let you wear this bracelet; he spent a lot of money on this."

We laughed as she put it on my wrist and as I checked my make-up in the vanity mirror. We had spent the whole day together, and I had a good time. We laughed, talked, joked, and even told each other some secrets. I could see our relationship was growing, and now that I was listening to her and being obedient to her words, I was getting a closer bond with her, a bond that only God could have created.

Mom had me turn around in a circle while she smiled proudly. "Mom, you act like this is my first Homecoming." Tears filled her eyes, and she grabbed a tissue off of my dresser.

"No, Sweetie, I just know it's your last." She walked out of the room.

I put on my shoes and sat on my bed. "Lord, thank you for bringing me this far. I love you, Father, and I praise you. You are my king and I glorify you with everything in me. Tonight, Father, cover me in your spirit, oh, God. Help me not to sin against you and to be pleasing in your sight. In Jesus name I pray, amen." Now, I was ready to have a good time.

CHAPTER 11

Step *in the name of Love, Groove in the name of love,"* played over the speakers as James and I grooved to the sultry beats of the DJ. The banquet hall where we had our Homecoming was breathtaking. A large chandelier hung above the walkway, and when we entered the actual hall, the tables were decorated with fresh cut flowers and candles. The colors for the Homecoming were dark purple, gold, and crème, and the theme was, "A Golden Year of Memories."

I was really excited when the DJ started playing old songs. He started with "She's a Brick House," then played "It's Like Candy" and ended his old school melody with a rendition of songs from Earth, Wind, and Fire. Only a few people came on the dance floor when the old songs were playing. Finally, the DJ started playing a whole bunch of rap songs and I decided to go get something to drink.

"Girl, you look cute; I like your dress!" Monique commented as we sat down.

"Thanks girl, your dress is cute, too; where did you get it from?"

"Lord and Taylor." She looked around and then said, "Eric told me he would meet me here because he had a surprise for me."

I stared at Monique in disbelief. "When did you and Eric start talking? You didn't tell me nothin' about it."

"Girl, please, when do you ever tell me anything about James?" She got me there. But I didn't feel that I had to spill my guts to her; besides, all James and I did was talk on the phone. Our relationship wasn't filled with drama and arguments, so there really wasn't anything to spill.

Monique hit me on the leg and we both looked at the door in aston-
ishment. Kristen walked in with a black cat suit on, with red stitching and
a drawstring pant bottom, some red and black Manolos, and a red and
black beret on her head. On her arm was none other than Oliver, with a
black and red pin stripe suit, red gators, and a black hat with red trim. It
just didn't get anymore ghetto than that. As she walked closer, I noticed
that she dyed her hair red and flipped it under the hat. Sometimes I wish
that we weren't related, though I wasn't surprised at her at all.

"Hey Kiva; how you?" She tried to yell over the music.

"Hey Kris; hey Oliver," I said unenthusiastically. He nodded at me
and pulled Kristen to the dance floor. She started freaking him down
and turned around and started backin' it up on him. He had his hands
up in the air bouncing to the music.

"I need to find another table," I told Monique and quickly got up.
James went to go talk to Nate and Alonzo while all this happened, so he
hadn't even seen them.

We found a table in the back and Monique and I started talking and
laughing about what people had on. Finally, Eric walked to our table and
bent down on one knee by Monique. Eric was the blackest boy I had ever
seen. Everyone told him he resembled Morris Chestnut and he did, but he
took it too far sometimes. He would try to sound like him and even lick
his lips like Morris. I guess when you got a good thing, you keep it going.

"Hey Babe, you wanna dance?" he asked while still on one knee.
Monique looked at me, smiled, and anxiously got up. "A.J., will you be
okay here by yourself?"

"Yeah, I'll be cool."

They went to the dance floor. I sat there not understanding why I was
here with the man of my dreams and we still hadn't been together for
five minutes alone except for the ride here. I scooted up to the table and
started playing with the flowers. I looked at the dance floor, wishing that
I was on it, but I couldn't find James.

"Alright y'all, I have a request from a James Richardson; this is for
you, Akiva," said the DJ.

Suddenly, Brian McKnight's song, "Back at One" came on over the
speakers. I smiled, stood up, and looked for him to come and get me. I sat
back down after standing on my toes and looking over the crowd for him.
Finally I started wondering if this was a trick he was playing. I started to

feel real bad until someone touched me on the shoulder. I turned around to see James standing there with his hand out.

"Can I have this dance, Akiva?"

I put my hand in his. He guided me to the dance floor, and I felt like we were the only people there, staring into each other's eyes and wishing that this moment could never end. I was so happy that I found him, and I thanked God every minute of it.

"You know, Kiva, I am so glad we finally hooked up." I smiled as I put my head on his shoulder.

"James, you are so sweet," I commented after a couple of minutes.

"Baby, you are the best thing that has ever happened to me, and I know we can make this last. You gotta be my one. I think about how much I think about you and how I want to be a better person because of you; it's only right." I had gotten so emotional and wanted to fall into his arms and have him carry me off the dance floor, but I knew it wouldn't be pretty.

"Now, Ladies and Gentlemen, we will announce the Homecoming Queen and King of this year's Homecoming dance." The announcer sounded really corny, and frankly, he ruined the mood that me and my James had going on. Everyone moved closer, whether they were taking pictures or not, while all the teachers gathered to the front of hall, which was right in front of the DJ's table. Mrs. Smith, who was head of the Homecoming committee, pulled out a beautiful crown from a box. It was filled with fake little diamonds encrusted all around it. Mr. Tyson, the gym teacher, brought the king's crown out of the box and pulled the flowers from behind the stage.

"Who do you think is gonna win this year?" Monique asked. I figured it was gonna be Shayla. Out of all the people who were running, she was the one that everyone knew. Even though her reputation wasn't the best, she at least had all the boys' votes.

"Probably Shayla, 'cause nobody really knows anyone else." I commented. Monique rolled her eyes and shook her head.

"You probably right, I mean it was only two people that ran against her. Who do you think is gonna win king?" I knew and she knew it was gonna be Eric. That whole week he had been passing out flyers and stickers and posters with his face pasted all over them; if he didn't win, I don't know who would have beat him. It was only two other boys running, and again, nobody knew who they were.

"I just know when Eric gets up there, Shayla better keep her hands to herself," said Monique. I laughed and leaned on her shoulder, trying to give my feet some relief.

"This year's Homecoming Queen is … Shayla Thompson!"

Everyone clapped while she walked up to receive her flowers and crown. She was so pretty. She was about my complexion, tall and thin with beautiful long flowing hair and perfect cheekbones. We often called her Janet Jackson, because she resembled her in the face. One thing I could say about Shayla was that she was the sweetest person I had ever met, and even though she tried to turn out my James, she was still cool with me, unlike half the population of Community Tech girls.

She had taken so many men and broken up so many relationships, you would have thought she was a regular home wrecker. But the way the relationships would end always made her look like the unsuspecting girl who wasn't even interested in the guy until he started buying her flowers and taking her out. It was never her fault, and that was her line for every girl who tried to confront her about stealing a man. No wonder Monique was so worried about Shayla touchin' all up on him; she had some kind of touch that these boys could not resist, and she used it at her disposal.

"Man, she looks really pretty tonight." I said.

"Who you telling," James commented. I looked at him, and he was in a daze, staring at her and her wave to the crowd. I hit him in the shoulder, and he grabbed me really quickly and kissed me on the cheek.

"But not as beautiful as my Kiva." He tickled me in my side, and I laughed as I pushed him away. Mrs. Smith grabbed the microphone from the DJ and announced the king.

"The King of this year's Homecoming is … Eric Clayson!" People applauded while he danced to the front of the stage. He was such a character. After they crowned him, he grabbed Shayla, picked her up, and kissed her on the cheek. I looked at Monique as she gave him the worst evil eye I had ever seen. I wanted to laugh, but I knew this wasn't one of those moments. After King Eric and Queen Shayla danced, the DJ started to play old songs again, and we decided to dance and be silly. We danced for about an hour or so and when we finally looked up, we noticed the only people on the dance floor were us and the teachers; everybody else was taking pictures, talking, or eating. Soon, couples started leaving.

When the dance was over, I was hungry. "Babe, can we go to a restaurant?" I whined as I got in the car.

"Hold on, Sweets, give me a minute." He was on the phone with Alonzo getting directions to his hotel room. I didn't want to go, but I figured that if we had to go, twenty or thirty minutes wouldn't kill me. He got off the phone and turned the ringer off.

"Now, you have my undivided attention, so where do you want to eat?"

"Well, Monique and Eric have reservations at Southern Expressions, so if you—"

"Babe, I wanna go somewhere we can be alone. How about we go to Sweet Agape? My uncle is a cook there, so I know he can get us some quick reservations." He had it all in the bag, and that was fine with me. Look at my man taking good care of me. He made the phone call, got reservations, and we cruised downtown. Sweet Agape was one of the nicest restaurants in Detroit; since the big renovation, Detroit was the place to go and the thing to do on the weekends.

We parked our car and walked hand in hand to the restaurant, where the concierge opened the door for us. As we walked in, the mix of jazz music and sweet barbecue smells tantalized my senses. The atmosphere was so calm and the dim lights gave a romantic yet jazzy setting, which was different from the noisy, crowded dance. I really liked the looks of this place and hoped for a good meal.

"Thirty dollars for some fried chicken!" I shouted to James. "We can go back to my house and my mama can fry us up some chicken for free." He laughed and put his menu down to get closer to my face.

"Sweetie, it's not your mother's cooking; that's why it's thirty dollars. Not saying your mother can't cook, but it's about presentation. Besides, it's more gourmet than it is southern cooking. Baby, just get what you want, don't worry about the price."

That's what I'm talking about, he knew my worth and was willing to pay for me to eat what I wanted. Clearly, his mama must have stuffed his pockets.

"I think I'll have the Cajun salmon with garlic mashed potatoes and steamed broccoli." He sounded so mature. The waitress looked at me, and I hoped that my meal measured up to his.

"I'll have the catfish with macaroni and cheese and greens. Oh yeah, and a side of cornbread." It sounded so much better in my head. He looked at me and smiled as I politely excused myself to go to the bathroom.

As I walked to the restroom, I felt this inadequacy come over me, making me feel as if I wasn't good enough for James. I mean he was so mature, well mannered, educated about Christ, and the best thing that ever happened to me since eyebrow arching.

I guess I had to come to terms with the fact that even though I wasn't perfect, I was working on being a better person, and besides, he wouldn't be with me if he thought that I wasn't at least close to his level. To me, it was just weird finally being with someone whom I could relate to. I've been saved my whole life, I was never out here clubbin', drinkin', smokin', or sexin'. I remember one time when I was about ten, these girls across the street pulled out a cigarette and a lighter and asked me did I want to smoke. I ran all the way home and never went over there again. When God said flee temptation, that's what I did.

But now the temptation is harder, and James knows what I'm going through. Sometimes I feel he knows me better than I know myself, which was always good. Even though we had only been together three weeks, we had known each other for four years, and we had been through so many of the same things. It had to be God's will. I couldn't see it any other way. I touched up my makeup, washed my hands, and brushed my hair into place. "Girl, you betta go out there and not be insecure about yourself; you are God's creation. When he made you, he broke the mold!" I spoke to myself. Sometimes I had to geek myself up, you know.

"You're back; how was your trip?" I laughed and thought about the fact that I was gone for a while; the waiter had brought our drinks, the bread, and the appetizer.

"Sorry, but I'm here now," I said throwing up my hands as he pulled out my chair and scooted it in for me.

"Yes, and I'm glad." He reached over the table and grabbed both of my hands.

"Kiva, I know you're probably tired of me saying this, but I just can't get enough of you. I know we've only been talking for about three weeks or so, but you are so beautiful, smart, full of energy and creativity, open-minded, and faithful."

My smile faded. "What do you mean by faithful?"

"Well, I mean even though we aren't together, you were still there for me like a girlfriend, you talked to me, chilled with me, and sacrificed time that could have been used elsewhere to spend with me."

I felt the guilt growing and building in me. I had to tell him, or at least let him know that he wasn't the only person in my life these past three weeks.

"Um, James I have to say something."

He put his finger over my mouth and reached for my chin and kissed me softly. "Kiva, I'm falling in love with you. I know it's soon, but I can't help it, being around you, and just wanting to love you. I just want to take care of you and love you like you're supposed to be loved."

My mind was still kissing him while he was talking. I had to bring myself back to reality for a moment. I couldn't tell him now. He just poured out his heart to me and I couldn't break his heart by telling him I went out with another guy.

I sat back in my seat and tried to think of how I could tell him without making it totally painful. "James, Baby, I care about you so much and I just wanted to tell you that."

"Food's here," he shouted with glee. The food smelled so good, I couldn't wait for the first taste. We prayed and dived in. Half way through, I remembered that I was going to tell him.

"James Baby, I—"

"Hold on, my phone is vibrating." He pulled his phone off his hip and answered it, already knowing who it was.

"Wassup man? We're at the restaurant now; we just got our food. What? That's sweet man; alright, we'll be over soon, one." I was not excited to hear what he was about to tell me.

"Nate said they messed up his room information. He was supposed to have a two-bed suite and instead they had given him a one-bed suite. Of course the one he paid for was more expensive, so the only room they had left was one of their penthouse suites, so that's where they're going now. He told me to call him when we're done so he can give me the room number and everything." A penthouse suite with over ten high school kids—I planned on not being there for long.

"That sounds nice; how long do we have to stay?" He laughed at me again, noticing the ounce of irritation in my voice.

"You don't wanna go?"

"I mean, it's cool, we can go, but I'm not trying to be there all night long is all I'm saying." He understood how I felt, and hopefully when he got around his boys, he would take that into consideration. I didn't want to be out until two o'clock in the morning and my parents knocking on my door tomorrow morning asking me what I was doing all night. I can't tell them I was at a hotel; how good does that sound?

"Well, I feel you." We both smirked at each other and tried to ignore the idea of us having sex for the first time together—him holding me and loving me in his arms—I couldn't even take the thoughts.

"So do you know what college you want to go to?" I asked, trying to quickly change the subject. "Well, I have been looking at a couple of schools, but I am still in prayer about where I should go." I wasn't at that level, but I guess I could be. That does make sense to actually ask God where did he want me to go; then it would be a lot easier for me, because he would provide everything.

"What about yourself?" He asked. "I know I'm trying to stay in state, but I'm still looking into it."

"Why in state? What if God wants you to go to Nebraska, or Atlanta, or South Carolina?"

"Well, I feel that God knows the desires of my heart, and he knows how much I love my family and how close I am to them, so pulling me out of my environment probably wouldn't be the best thing for me personally."

"That's true, but you also have to understand that God may need you to step out of your comfort zone to touch some lives that you never thought you would touch. Everything that God wants us to do is not comfortable. If we could do it without him, we wouldn't need him. Not saying God wants to move you, but just opening your eyes so that if he does, you can be obedient."

Man, if I could hear him drop those words of encouragement and knowledge all the time, I would. He showed me something new every day, and even when I didn't feel like listening to his lessons, I still ended up learning. He taught me so much about life, love, God, and how to just be a better woman. Sometimes though, I felt as if I wasn't as much of an influence.

"James, do you think that I am an asset to your life?" He looked up from his plate in confusion.

"What do you mean? Like, do I feel that you bring more value to my life or that you help me grow in various ways?"

"Duh, yeah."

"Kiva, you are one of the most mature females I know. And I mean not just as far as education, but Christ, which is most important, school, and life period. When I ask you questions you can always back it up with something from the Word, which I find attractive and very clever of you. Girl, you light up my life."

I felt better now. After about twenty minutes of conversation and good food, I knew it was getting pretty late. "You ready to go? I'm pretty full."

He paid the bill, pulled my seat out, put on my jacket, put on his, and we were off.

CHAPTER 12

When we reached the hotel, it was a mad house. We heard the party all the way down the hall. The place was huge. It had a living room with a big screen TV and a bar, with two huge rooms off the living room. The walls were a light pink and the carpet was plush and cream. It was beautiful, but I knew this was not my environment.

"Wassup y'all!" Nate shouted as he walked into the living room. He had shed the suit and tie for a t-shirt and some jeans; he planned to be here awhile. He had already claimed one of the bedrooms; five minutes later, Natalie walked out with a t-shirt on and some sleep shorts. I guess we were the only two just stopping by. "Hey girl," Natalie screamed in my ear. You could tell that she had been drinking and that she was more than tipsy.

"Hey, uh, Natalie, you okay" I asked, sounding concerned.

"Yeah, I'm fine. Me and Nate staying here tonight. I just hope my mama don't call my cell. Then I might get into some big trouble." She threw her hand out and almost fell off the couch. She jerked herself forward and laughed.

"Natalie, how much did you drink?"

"How you know I was drinking, and what you wanna know for?" She said with an attitude.

"I just want to make sure you're—"

"Oh, I see it; preacher girl want some, huh? Well, ain't none left; me and Nate drank the whole bottle of Vodka. We mixed it with Cranberry juice, and it was good."

"No Natalie, I don't want any; I just—"

"I can see if Nate has something else in his car." She got up and realized that she couldn't walk so instead she yelled across the living room to where James and Nate were talking.

"Nate, you got any more alcohol, 'cause Kiva smelled it on my breath and said it smelled like it tasted good, so could she have some." I felt like everybody there turned and looked at me in shock.

"Nate she's drunk, I don't drink and I don't want anything to drink."

"Whatever," Natalie said after finally getting her balance. "Heifer, don't call me drunk and don't act like you too good to drink, 'cause I know what you said, and I ain't no liar!" She yelled in my face, barely keeping her balance.

"Natalie, calm down. I don't want anything to drink. I just want you to sit down and calm down."

"Don't tell me to do nothin'. You ain't my mama." By that time she was causing a scene and Nate pulled her into the bedroom.

"Babe, you okay?" James hugged me from behind.

"No, I want to go home," I said angrily.

"Okay, we'll go." After about twenty minutes of him running around looking for Nate and Alonzo to take a picture, we finally left. By the time I got home, it was about 1:30 and I was ready to fall out. What an evening it was. I had a good time with James and my friends, and a bad experience with others. I knew we shouldn't have gone to the hotel, but the night was over. I was glad, and so were my feet.

✝✝✝✝✝

"Ring, ring." It was 9 o'clock in the morning and everyone decided not to answer the phone. I tried covering my head with the pillow; when that didn't work, I reached for the phone.

"Hello," I said in the most unpleasant voice I could find.

"Good morning, Sweetheart, how are you?" As soon as I heard his voice, my whole demeanor changed.

"Hey James, how are you?" I said in a sweet voice.

"I could tell you just woke up, but I wondered if you wanna go to breakfast with me this morning." A big smile came across my face.

"Of course I would, but you have to give me about 45 minutes to an hour to get ready."

"That's fine. I'll just pick you up at ten; is that cool?"

"Yeah, that sounds fine. I'll see you then."

"One." I hung up the phone and jumped out of the bed, skipping to my closet. This was probably the day he was going to ask me to be his girlfriend. I mean it's the perfect setting—morning, breakfast—you know, perfect timing. As I ran into the bathroom to run my shower, my mother caught me in mid leap.

"Why are you so happy?"

"James and I are going to breakfast this morning, and he'll be here in an hour." I was so proud of that. I brought my towel and washcloth into the bathroom and went through my usual routine. Finally, I picked out an outfit. It had to be something cute so that when we told our kids about the beginning of our relationship, he could describe what I had on verbatim and comment on how cute it was, and how he'll never forget that day.

I chose a sheer brown shirt with a brown tank underneath and some brown shoes. I put on a brown and silver choker and touched up my hairstyle from the night before. I threw on some jeans and added some dainty brown earrings, heart shaped. I was cute and ready to go. Just as I walked down the stairs, he rang the doorbell.

"Hey Baby, you look real nice."

"Thanks, you look like … well, you look nice, too." All of a sudden, I felt over dressed. He wore some jeans, a white polo shirt, his chain, and a black Nike baseball cap. He looked like he was going to work out and I looked like I was going on a date.

"You should have told me what to wear; I'm gonna go change."

"No, don't change." He grabbed my arm as I turned around. "You look good, just keep what you have on." I grabbed my coat and hat and we left. As we got in the car, he immediately turned off the radio.

"I want to talk to you."

"Wassup," I said, excited.

"Well, you know I love you, right?"

"Yes, and I love you, too."

"I just want to let you know that these past three or four weeks have really been a blessing. You are a blessing, and I am glad to have you here in my life." I smiled and turned toward him, waiting for the big question.

"I feel the same way, James. You have really made me a better person, and you know I just want to be better for God and for you." I rubbed his arm. He nodded and smiled.

"I mean, you've been honest and faithful to me. You've never lied to me, and I know I can trust you." That's when my smile went down. I knew it was gonna catch up with me soon.

"Babe, you know these past weeks, I haven't thought about anyone but you, and haven't seen anyone but you. I couldn't tear myself away from thinking about you and just wanting to be around you. How about you?" I was caught off guard.

"Um, yeah I thought about you the whole time." I leaned back in my seat.

"Have you seen anyone else?"

"Well, I went out with one guy, but it didn't mean anything."

"Of course, 'cause you probably met him before me and just had to get him out of your system, right?" I slowly shook my head.

"So you met him after me, and then after we got serious you didn't have any contact with him?" I shook my head again.

"So what happened with him?" He sounded a little angry. The words slowly but surely came flowing out of my mouth.

"Well, we went out on a date, and we went to his boys' house, but his crazy ex-girlfriend was there, so I had to hide upstairs until she left. Then after she left, we went out to eat."

James pulled up into a huge parking lot and found a spot where no cars were.

"Did you kiss him?"

"Huh?"

"Did you kiss him?" His voice got louder.

"Yes," I said quietly.

"So you mean to tell me that after all the attention and affection I gave you, you was still out here with another guy? And you kissed him. You went to some boys' house that you didn't know and chilled there. How old was he?

"Twenty-two."

"Twenty-two! What you think that nigga wanted from you, a friend-ship? I see where you are, man. I thought we was on the same level."

"We are, James; I mean, I just made a mistake."

"You made a mistake kissin' that nigga and goin' out on a date with him! When did you go?" I was sinking myself deeper and deeper into my seat.

"Thursday."

"What, you played me right before Homecoming? You straight up shady! I thought you was way better than that, man. What was all that stuff about you loving me and wanting to be with me? I thought I was the one you wanted to spend the rest of your life with?"

"James, you were the one telling me you wanted to marry me, but you haven't even asked me to be your girlfriend, how do you think that makes me feel?" I looked him dead in his eyes.

"Kiva, we still getting to know each other, why would I rush into that? I'm not tryin to waste time with a person that's playin' games!" I rolled my eyes and sat back in my seat.

"James, we have known each other for four years, how much more do we need to know about each other?" He chuckled and took his seat belt off.

"Well, now I know that you're a liar, and you don't think about no one but yourself. Kiva, I couldn't think about kickin' it with no one else during this time because I wanted to focus on you, but you out here going out on dates, that makes me think like you not serious?"

"James, if I wasn't serious, would I be here?"

Kiva, if you were serious, you wouldn't of went out with that dude."

We sat there in silence.

"James, look-"

"Get out my car!" I didn't move. Was he serious?

"Get out my car, Kiva. Ain't nobody playing wit you!" He unlocked the door and I jumped out. He sped off as soon as I closed the door. I walked next door to the Taco Bell and sat on the steps. I was so embarrassed and ashamed and tired of myself. It was all my fault. Why did I let myself get this deep?

I cried and held myself in the cold, thinking about my next move. If I called my dad, he would hunt that boy down. If I called Kristen, she would laugh at me the whole way home. Ananda and Monique were at work, and my brother was probably out frolicking with Jessica. Guess I had to take the bus.

As I stood up, I pushed my hair behind my ears and wiped my tears. The wind blew against my face, and my eyes watered because of the coldness and the pain, from the wind and from James. The light snow that had fallen was sticking to the bottom of my boots, making it hard to walk toward the bus stop. As soon as I got there, James came rolling around the corner.

"Look, I'm sorry; get back in, so we can talk." I ignored him and began to search through my purse for a dollar.

"Akiva, you hear me? Come on, get in the car," he yelled.

"James, I don't have anything to say to you because I told you the truth and you bit my head off. I ain't got time for that."

"Akiva, I already knew. Kristen told me Friday before school because the guy you were with was on the phone with her boyfriend after everything happened, and he mentioned that you were there. She wanted to know if we were still going to Homecoming." I looked at him in shock and disbelief.

"Why should I believe that? Why would Kristen do that to me?" I asked with an attitude.

"Will you get in the car?"

"Only if you take me straight home." He agreed. As we rode back to my house, I didn't say a word. He was mad at me, but he had to understand that he could have handled it in a different way. Don't make a plan to take me out to eat, have me dress up, and kick me out of the car to show me a lesson.

When I got home, I walked in the house like nothing happened. I was cool, calm, and ready to cut Kristen's head off. I hopped up the stairs and ran into my room to call Kristen. I threw my purse and coat into my rocking chair. The phone rang before I could make my call.

"Hello."

"Hey girl, it's Monique. What's goin on wit cha?" Good, at least it wasn't for my mom; I could get Monique off the phone easily.

"Hey 'Nique. Look, I'm gonna have to call you back because I have to take care of some business."

"Alright, I just wanted to know if you wanted to go to the mall with me later, 'cause I'm bored."

"Yeah, that's cool. Call me when you're ready." I hung up and called Kristen immediately. I sat on the bed nervous and skeptical; wondering why she would do that to me, and if she didn't, why would he lie.

"Hello."

"Hi Aunty Deborah; is Kristen in?"

"Yes, she just walked in the door. She went out to get groceries to cook me breakfast; wasn't that sweet?"

"Yes, it was, Aunty." Kristen came on the line.

"Hey wassup, Kiva?" She talked like she hadn't just sold me out to my future husband.

"Hey Kris, what you doin' tonight?"

"Nothin' why?"

"Oh, I just wanted to know. You goin' out with Oliver?"

"Probably, yeah, but I know him and Alex probably want to do something, too; maybe we can double date," she said sarcastically. I laughed and knew what I was going to do at that moment.

"Look, I'm not gonna protect your man anymore. I saw him at the movies last week with some girl, and they was all hugged up." She was silent. "Hello?"

"You a liar. You just mad because I told James about you and Alex goin' out, and now since he kicked you to the curb, you gonna try to break up my relationship!"

"Whatever, Kristen. James didn't kick me to the curb. Don't you worry about me and James, that has nothing to do with you."

"So then, why you calling me about my man and lying on him"

"Kristen, I'm not lying." She sat on the phone in silence for a minute and you could hear her sniffle.

"So why didn't you tell me when you saw Oliver?"

"'Cause I was lookin' out for you. I figured you would find out anyway, and I wouldn't have to be the bearer of bad news."

"Ain't no bad news, 'cause he ain't a cheater or a liar."

"Oh yeah, he's just a thug who likes girls ten years younger than him and sells weed. Give me a break, just for a minute okay, girl? He don't love you; he just like that free stuff in between your legs." She sniffled some more and at that moment my heart softened.

"Kristen, you okay?" She acted like she didn't hear me, and the sniffles turned into full-fledged tears.

"Look Kristen, I didn't mean to go off, but you know that man ain't no good." I could tell she was trying to hide the tears, and I began to feel terrible for what I said. When they said the truth hurts, they weren't lying.

"Kiva, don't worry about me and Oliver, we gonna be fine. We just have some things to work out. Maybe I'm not spending enough time with him."

"Kristen, it doesn't matter. I mean, if he loves you, he loves you, and you don't need to change who you are so that he won't cheat. That's crazy, and you know it."

"But I love him. Why would he do that to me?" She sounded sorrowful.

"I don't know, Kristen. That's something only he can answer." We were both quiet for a minute. I didn't know what to say or what to do. All I could think of was to encourage her to feel better and to think about herself now.

"Cousin," she said sounding five-years-old. "Yes?"

"Can you come over? I feel like having company." I smiled and thought about the last time she had called me cousin, when we were about ten.

"Sure, cousin, no problem. I'll be over in a minute."

"Oh yeah, and Kiva?"

"Yes?"

"I'm sorry about you and James. I was just jealous because you guys looked so cute at Homecoming and Oliver bought me that outfit to wear, so I had to wear it." We both laughed as we got off the phone.

CHAPTER 13

CALLED OUT

The air was crisp and cool. Watching all the leaves swirl around in the wind with the light snow as they fell to the ground made me wish that it stayed this way all year round.

I exchanged my skirt for some jeans and my boots for my black Nikes. I threw on a black baseball cap, my big hoop earrings, and my black waist length down coat. I walked to Kristen's house a block away and went to the side door because I knew how Aunty is about using the front door when it's not a special occasion.

Her house was bigger and prettier than my parents'. My aunty was divorced and now five years later, she was healed from that relationship and engaged to another man. I liked Fred, though. He was good to her, and he was saved. He was always the perfect gentleman.

I rang the doorbell and immediately heard their Yorkshire terrier, Butterscotch, barking at the door. He was the cutest dog I had ever seen.

"Move, Butters!" I heard Kristen yell. She opened the door and pulled me into the house. I almost tripped over the steps as she pulled me into the living room where Aunty Deborah and Fred were watching television.

"Hey Aunty Deborah, hey Fred," I waved quickly, and they waved back.

We ran up the spiral staircase and walked down the hallway to her room. Kristen's room was laid out. She had a queen size canopy bed, which was pink and white, with satin sheets; the carpet was plush and pink. Her dresser was cream and her walls were cream with pink flowers and floating ribbons. Her closet had a mirror on the door and slid open to reveal a walk-in closet with a rotating rack. It was nice, and she decorated it all. She was good at interior design.

She was also the best artist in the world. On her wall were pictures of drawings her mother framed: horses riding off into the sunset, a woman looking at herself in the mirror, and a group of friends out to eat. She was talented, and the world was waiting on her to explode. What I didn't understand was how a person so bitter about everything could draw so many beautiful pictures, including sketches of people living happy, pain-free lives.

When I looked to the left, I saw on her easel the beginning of a picture. It was a woman on her knees, with her head up and her hands outstretched, obviously praising God. She was on a stage, and the audience was clapping and praising her. She had a pencil and pad in front of her, a Bible next to her, and a microphone next to the Bible. From her facial expressions, she looked like she was in pain, and it seemed like the audience didn't see that; all they saw was her.

"Wow, Kristen, this is nice."

"Thanks, do you get it?" I looked at her as if she asked me a stupid question.

"Well, apparently she's famous. All these people are praising her and believe that she has a gift. To me she looks tired and drained. Like they drained all her energy."

Kristen picked up her pencil and pointed out things in the picture to me.

"She's in pain, but it's different. She was a chosen one of God. God gave her talents and gifts to share with the world, and she used them for her gain. No one sees God in her. She's alone and even when she cries out to God for help, it seems like the crowd cries out for more of her. She worked her way to the top, and now she's ready to give it up, to walk into what God has for her: joy, peace, and love. The audience could never supply her with those things. I mean she truly feels that it doesn't profit a man to gain the whole world and lose his soul. That's why this picture is called Matthew 16:26."

I stood there in awe of the explanation. Kristen was so deep about this picture, and even though she wasn't doing right all the time, her mind was still focused on Christ in certain ways.

"I mean, Kiva I have so many dreams, and so many things I want to accomplish. Even though I haven't been living right, God wants me to do certain things for his kingdom, and I can't turn away from it. No matter how hard I've tried to not have this calling on my life, I have no choice but to walk in it. I just feel like if I give up all the things I'm doing right now, I'm gonna miss out on something." She sat on her bed and tried to close her eyes so that the tears wouldn't flow.

"Kristen, be glad that God has awesome plans for you, plans to prosper you, and make you whole, plans to give you wealth and knowledge beyond your wildest dreams. God is going to use you to touch other lives and bring others into the kingdom of heaven." I sat next to her and held her close.

"I have done so much wrong, though. How could God ever forgive me for walking out of his will and disrespecting him?" She looked up at me in confusion and fear.

"That's why he's God, because he's able to give you a second, third, or fourth chance. You don't have to work your way back into his arms; you can ask him to forgive you. Where's your Bible?" She pointed to her desk and I pulled out the Bible.

"Look, 1 John 1:9 says, *'If we confess our sins, he is faithful and just to forgive us our sins, and to cleanse us from all unrighteousness.'* So don't think that when you ask for forgiveness and you repent, which means to turn away, that God won't forgive you. He still loves you; you just have to trust him and believe in him."

"Don't worry about having to be perfect for him; he's not after a perfect person but after a perfect heart, which produces perfect praise and worship. What more could he ask for? Worship him and love him; he is your savior and friend, and he loves you unconditionally. In him, you will never lack; he will make you whole because his love is everlasting, enduring, and pure. Believe me girl, I know. This whole Alex thing was so stupid of me, and I could have put myself in a bad situation, but I'm stronger, and better for it."

Kristen got up and grabbed a tissue off her dresser. "Kiva, I'm done with Oliver, for real this time. I'm sorry for all the mean things I've said to you, and for being a jerk sometimes, I guess I was just trying to make myself feel better. It's like you never do anything wrong, so when I found out about Alex, I was happy that you were messing up because it made me feel better, you know?"

I sat there kind of confused.

"I will say this Kristen, I was wrong for going out with the man. I should have never betrayed James' trust, or even given Alex the impression that we were gonna kick it. More importantly, put myself in a position where I knew God didn't want me to go. But that is why we are human, we make mistakes, we learn from them and we get better."

She smiled at me and gave me a hug.

"Kiva, you know everything, don't you!"

"No Kristen, I just know who my redeemer is."

CHAPTER 14

You know, Kiva, I always knew in the back of my mind that Oliver had other chicks on the side."

"How you figure?"

"I mean, we hardly ever spent time together unless we were sexin', and when we did go out, Alex or one of his other boys was there. He never showed me any affection in front of his boys and never really took an interest in me or what I wanted out of life. Those conversations about getting married came up, but it was only when we were about to have sex."

I felt really bad for Kristen. I felt bad because she was missing out on the true lover of her soul, Jesus. We as women always try to replace God with a man, and spend all of our time and energy focusing on him, myself included. But when I started to realize that God wants to be with me first and establish a relationship with me, it made me understand why. How can I learn to love a man, if I can't love and appreciate my creator?

When I really start to think about God's goodness, I just reflect on the fact that this is the same God who spoke to Moses, the same God who spoke to David, and the same God who changed Paul. All of these were great people, and God talks to me as well. How incredible is that, of all the people in the world, he talks to little old me, just another girl who lives in Detroit?

"Girl, that's why God is delivering you from him."

"I know, so I can meet a real man. I don't have time for little boys."

I looked at her wondering what she was thinking.

"Girl, haven't you had enough?"

"I mean, I just like having a guy around, you know? It's different for you 'cause you got a father in the house, and a brother. All I got is me."

"That may be true, but you have to understand that God is probably separating you two so that he can get closer to you. He wants to bless you more and cultivate your gifts and talents for his kingdom, and you need to lean on him more before you lean on another man."

Kristen was quiet, and I hoped she was thinking about what I said.

✝✝✝✝✝

Ring, ring …

"Hello,"

"Hey, what's up?" James asked. Wow, that's how long my day had been. I had completely forgotten about earlier.

"Hey," I said lightly, hoping he wouldn't take it as standoffish.

"Um, I was wondering if I could come see you tonight, because I need to talk to you about some things." At first I thought it would be a good idea, since my parents didn't care if I had company when they weren't home, but then I didn't think it would be appropriate.

"Well, my parents aren't home right now, so maybe we could go somewhere and talk, as long as you promise to not kick me out of the car." I laughed and he chuckled, embarrassed and surprised that I made the comment.

"You know that's cool; in about how long?"

"Well, give me about an hour or so, I need to take care of some business."

"Alright then." We hung up and immediately I got excited. I decided to do some homework before he came so that I could have some work accomplished over the weekend. I sat down at my desk, tossed in a jazz CD, and began working. Five minutes into my work, I heard the doorbell ring, and Justin ran out of his room to answer it. I decided to be nosy and listen at the stairs. He opened the door and as I sat on the steps, I could vaguely see her, everything but her face. She had on some of the tightest jeans I had ever seen in my life tucked into brown snakeskin boots. She had on a black waist jacket with a fur hood and a brown and black purse.

"Hey Baby," she said seductively, hugging Justin. She was a mess.

"Wassup girl," he replied, taking her coat off. Oh, I was staying here if they were staying here.

"So what are we going to do tonight?" She walked into the library, which gave me a better view of her.

"We're gonna go and get something to eat, and then come back here and chill."

"But Baby," she said putting her arms around him and pulling him close. "I wanted to be alone tonight, just me and you." How much more could she throw herself at my brother? I was getting sick.

"I know Baby, but my sister is here…"

"But if we—"

"Justin!" I called his name before she could even finish her sentence.

"Yes," he yelled.

"Could you come here?" He ran up the stairs reluctantly and walked in my room.

"What do you want?"

"When are you and Jessica leaving because I need some peace and quiet;" He stepped back from the door and stared.

"Kiva, whatever, I don't know."

He walked away and went downstairs. A couple of minutes later, they were walking out the door. I was glad they were gone. I continued to get back to my work as the hour zoomed by. I couldn't believe how much work I got done. By the time I was finished and getting myself ready, James called.

"Hello," I said sweetly.

"Hey, you ready?" I sat there looking at myself in the mirror and putting on makeup.

"Yes, I'm almost there," I said.

"Good, I'll be there in about fifteen minutes." I went downstairs and grabbed an apple from the kitchen while I waited. I just hoped my brother was safe. He was out with that girl, and I didn't trust her. I was still trying to understand why he was with her and why he was dealing with her. I moved to the living room and sprawled myself on the couch. I sat up in the darkness of the room and saw the little branches of light shining through the blinds. The light shot shadows and shapes on the piano and bounced off the mirror above it. As James pulled into the driveway, the lights from his car bounced from the right side of the room to the left side, brightening the whole area up. I walked to the door and opened it, anticipating the doorbell.

"Hi," I said.

"How are you?" He had a single rose in his hand. It wasn't Alex's dozen, but at least his wasn't in vain.

"Thank you so much," I said taking it from him and putting it up to my nose to smell. It was fully bloomed and had the most wonderful fragrance to it.

"Can I sit down?"

"Sure, if you want." I went to go put the flower in some water, and returned to him laying back on the couch like he lived here. "Excuse me, sir, don't get too comfortable." He sat up immediately.

"Oh, I was just chillin'. So did you want to leave or stay?"

"Well, we can stay for a minute, but then we need to leave, because I just wouldn't feel comfortable or appropriate for us to be here by ourselves."

"Well, Kiva, I apologize for confronting you the way I did."

I was trying not to smirk and get excited, I just sat there and let him talk.

"I should have sat you down and talked to you like an adult. It's just that I'm feelin' you and I felt like you played me."

I scooted closer to him on the couch and sat back.

"James, I'm sorry, it was really not my intention to play you. I've known you for four years and I am glad we kickin' it like this, I guess – honestly, I don't know what I was thinking." I messed up, and it will never happen again."

We hugged and he scooted back from me.

"That leads me to my next question."

I was hoping he was going to ask me what I thought he was going to ask. I wanted to be official so bad.

"Kiva, I think we need to slow down and really spend more time getting to know each other. I think that we were rushing into this, and that if you really like me the way you say you do, we can both spend the time to learn more about what each other wants, and really decide if we want to go further with this relationship, what do you think?"

How devastated was I. Back to square one.

CHAPTER 15

Shout *for the victory, shout if you been set free, shout ...*" The choir was off the hook this morning. Our church was known for our Young Angelics choir, young adults between the ages of 13 and 19. Ananda was one of the best singers in the choir, and they were talking about moving her up to the older women's choir because of her voice, but I knew she liked being the center of attention in this choir.

"Afternoon, saints. We thank God for you this glorious afternoon. Holy is the name of the Lord."

Sister Davenport was about to make church announcements. She was what the children's church called "LW" or long winded. She could talk for hours and hours on end about anything; good thing she was working for the church, 'cause she sure was teaching me the spirit of patience.

"This week, we will be having our annual Thanksgiving drive, so bring all of your canned goods and nonperishable items to the church office. Also, on Thanksgiving morning, we will be having service with our sister church, Blessed Temple on Schaefer and Six mile. Service starts at 10:30 a.m."

Good, I get to see James on Thanksgiving; that's something to be thankful for.

"Also, we will be having our annual women's conference, entitled 'Women who pray', which will be held here the first week of November. You don't want to miss the awesome speakers that will be present. Get your ticket and t-shirt and join us for a week filled with blessed women of God progressing in his words, moving in his spirit, and worshipping in his love. Don't miss it." She was done. That was truly the grace of God.

Now I had to go to the bathroom. I got up slowly from the row and walked toward the door. As soon as I got to the exit, the usher told me to go sit back down.

"Ma'am, I really, really have to go to the bathroom."

"After the choir sings their next selection, you can go." I smiled politely and sat in the last row, hoping Ananda would sing her solo, because that's the only reason I was not bustin' through that door. The choir stood up and Ananda came to the front. All I heard was the kids in the youth department screamin', *"Sang girl, you betta let God use you!"*

The piano started to play and right after that the organ chimed in. The choir started rocking back and forth, and a couple of people stood up already knowing the song she was about to sing.

"Glory and power, oh God, Blessings and honor, oh God, dominion for-ever..." The choir chimed in after a couple of bars and I had to stand up. As I listened to the choir praise God, I couldn't do anything but lift my hands and praise him as well. He had been so good to me; no matter how many situations I put myself in, he still took care of me.

I was never the one to get all excited when somebody could sing well. I guess my mother always instilled in me that anybody can sing, but it takes more than just a voice to effectively minister the word of God, and our choir was usually excellent at doing that. As I stood there in his pres-ence, feeling his spirit on me, I couldn't help but be thankful that God loved me so much. I raised my hands higher and closed my eyes to focus on his goodness. A couple minutes later, he dropped a scripture into my spirit, I Corinthians 2:9:

> *"But it is written, eye hath not seen, nor ear heard, neither have entered into the heart of man, the things which God hath pre-pared for them that love him."*

What does that mean to me? Was I going to be great in the ministry and make an impact on people's lives? I dropped down in my seat and medi-tated on the verse and what I thought it meant, then I asked God, and he answered, *"You're not ordinary but an extraordinary child of mine. You have gifts in you that no one else has."*

I stood there eating on his words and just comprehending what he was telling me. It was hard to believe that of all the people in the world,

I was called of God, called to do bigger and better things. I sat in church looking up and smiling, thanking and praising God for choosing me to do his work.

The choir went into a reprise of "Breathe on Me" by John P. Kee, and immediately, I broke into tears. I couldn't contain my emotions. I mean, when I think of all the things I've been through and how disobedient I've been and for him to still say, "You are my child and you are extraordinary," is amazing to me. For someone to forgive and forgive and still bless is beyond my comprehension.

His word says that he calls me friend, and that we're co-heirs to the throne of Jesus Christ, so how can I turn down an offer to live eternally in his presence? All I have to do is follow his will and lean on him, and when I get weak, his strength is made perfect in my weakness. So really, what is the problem? He is waiting to bless me.

The choir sat down and the pastor came up in the midst of people still praying and worshipping. They played the music really low as the pastor got on the microphone "Oh God, we honor you today, Hallelujah to the king of kings, the lord of Lords. He's my savior, my Lord, and my best friend! If you know what I'm talking about, shout unto the Lord!"

By this time, people were in the aisles praising his name, clapping and jumping up and down, just thanking God. When I was younger, I never understood why people did that, but now that I'm older, and I see how God has moved through my life, through all the mistakes and mess-ups and yet still blesses me, I know that he is worth praising every day and every night.

I think a lot of people my age take for granted what they have. For example, you didn't have to be born in the United States, or even in a middle class family, for that matter. You could be living in a third world country starving to death, or living on the street. You could even be living in a country where you couldn't practice your religion for fear of death. How blessed are you? We get so caught up on things that are carnal, like clothes, hair, what he or she thinks about me, but those things aren't as important as our relationship with Christ.

I thought of II Corinthians 4:17 –18, which says,

> For our light affliction, which is but for a moment, worketh for
> us a far more exceeding and eternal weight of glory. While we

look not at the things which are seen, but at the things which
are not seen: for the things which are seen are temporal; but
the things which are not seen are eternal.

In other words, we as Christians, and as human beings period, focus on what we see, but we have to understand that when God takes away or adds something to our lives, it is for a greater purpose, to edify us and help us grow in what he needs us to be for his kingdom. If we look at the situation with carnal eyes, it may look bad, but if we stand on the promises that God has for us, he will bless us.

Didn't he say, *"Prove that I will not open the windows of heaven and pour you out a blessing that there shall not be room enough to receive it"?* He helps us in our time of need: *"For I will dwell in and among you and be your God."* He keeps us from hurt harm or danger, *"For he shall give his angels charge over thee, to keep thee in all thy ways. They shall bear thee up in their hands, lest thou dash thy foot against a stone."*

God truly protects us, and when we start to understand how much he values us as his children, we will value ourselves more, knowing who we are in Christ Jesus, victorious, more than a conqueror, and his workmanship created in Christ Jesus unto good works. I can do anything through him. What an awesome God we serve.

Pastor started his sermon entitled, "Show Me Your Fruit." He talked about what type of fruit people bear and how we should be careful about who we hang around and what we do 'cause we don't wanna kill our witness, in so many words. He made it so much more concise and clear when he preached. After service, I finally got to go to the bathroom, and when I came out, Ananda was standing next to the door.

"Hey girl, you really let God move through you today. Man, that song really ministered to me."

"Thank you, girl, but like you said, God gets all the glory. I saw you back there, praying up a storm; you must have a lot to be thankful for."

"Girl, you know how I do."

"Alright Lady, where we goin' to eat?"

✞✞✞✞✞

"Y'all goin' to eat with us?" My mother yelled out of the window.

"Mom, we waited over an hour for Dad; why wouldn't we?" She gave me the look, and I quickly got in the car. Ananda started the engine, and we were off.

I sat in her car listening to the radio and wondering what my brother was doing. He usually doesn't miss church.

"I wonder if they're gonna go pick up Justin," I said. Ananda was engrossed into the song. Her head was bobbing back and forth and she was trying to do all the runs he was doing in the songs.

"Girl, your parents are hungry, and knowing your dad, he probably said call him, which means when your mom asks him, he's gonna say no, and then we'll be on our way." Ananda was right. We jumped on 96 and twenty minutes later pulled up near the Mall. We parked by the restaurant, grabbed our purses, and walked in.

"Ma'am, it'll be about a fifteen minute wait." We all sat down and waited for our name to be called. The aroma of the pasta and garlic bread floated around the restaurant. I sat back against the wall and smoothed out my skirt. My shoes were still shiny, but my feet were killing me. If I were at home, I would have taken them off about an hour ago.

I noticed Ananda was on the phone with her boyfriend. She had her legs crossed, her purse in her lap and a big smile on her face. She got on my nerves. She and Jeff seemed like a match made in heaven. They never fought, they prayed together, and they were just alike in every way. They had the same style of dress, the same perceptions of things, and the same ideas about things. It was scary; my parents weren't even like that, and they've been married for over 20 years.

"Party of four for Niran, party of four for Niran." I was the first one up. I motioned to my parents and Ananda. As we followed him to the table, Ananda and I walked behind him. He sat our placemats out nicely and asked if we wanted any water. We ordered, ate and went our separate ways, me with Ananda and my parents together. I was spending the rest of the day with my girl, and maybe even doing a little shopping.

CHAPTER 16

iing!" Lunch time, finally. Most of the time, kids skipped school to grab something to eat or just left for the rest of the day, but I was a good one; I had never skipped. I decided to just suffer through the days with our horrible school lunches. I walked in the lunchroom with a bag of chips I got from the vending machine, some fruit snacks, and a pop. It wasn't healthy, but it was better than that nasty tuna surprise they were having for lunch.

I saw Kristen sitting at the table with her friend Nakiya. I really didn't feel like hearing the life and times of Nakiya Simpson, so I looked for another table. I saw Monique with Eric. I waved at her and she gave me the look as if to not come over, then she pointed to James who was coming into the lunchroom in the opposite doorway. He looked so good. As he sauntered over toward me, his brown Timberlands slapped against the hard granite floor. He had on a brown sweater and blue jeans with brown stitching. I saw him this morning with the matching Cleveland Browns cap to match, and he looked even better. I liked the way he dressed; he was just so fine!

"Hey Sweetie, you plan on sittin' with me for lunch?"

"Why I would love to sit with you. Where do you want to sit?" I asked innocently.

"You lead, I'll follow." I walked over to the corner of the lunchroom and we pulled up two chairs to a vacant table. He didn't have anything to eat and looked like he didn't even realize it was lunch, just another break in the middle of his day. That's why he was so skinny.

"You not hungry?" I asked while opening my bag of chips.

He sat back in his chair and looked nervous. "Naw, I'm straight. I'll eat after school." He sat up on the table and looked me in my eyes.

"Kiva, you know I love you, right?"

"I mean, yeah, we talked about it before." He scooted closer to me and grabbed the chips out of my hand.

"Well, Kiva I just want you to know that since I met you, I haven't thought about anyone else. I think about you all the time and I care about you so much. How do you feel about me?" I was caught off guard with his question. He was in the middle of wooing me; why would he ask me something like that?

"James, you know you are the only person I want to be with, and I can't imagine spending my time with anyone else. I can say that you are my friend and my love interest. I guess I never understood that until I met you. We have been through a lot of ups and downs these past four months, but we have been able to talk through things and work it out." He sat there rubbing his hands together with a smile on his face. He then pulled out a red velvet-looking box.

"I bought this for you. Merry Christmas."

"Boy, Christmas passed!" I hit him on the arm. I opened the box and in it was a charm bracelet with three charms on it. One of the charms was a heart and it said "My first love"; the second charm was a Bible that had the verse, 1 John 4:18 on it, and the third charm was a pair of dance shoes. As I picked it up, my eyes widened at the surprise. I didn't even know what to say.

"James, I … thank you so much!" I stood up and hugged him and he sat back down and put on my bracelet.

"Let me explain each charm." He gently pulled my arm toward him. "The first charm I picked was a heart, and it said my first love, because I remember you telling me that even though you've had other relationships before, I was someone that you truly loved, and your first. Then I picked the dance shoes because I know it's something that you love." I couldn't stop smiling.

"So why did you get the Bible with that verse in it? I don't know what it is."

"Kiva, this verse says that perfect love casteth out all fear, and to me it means a lot. The reason why I haven't committed to anyone is because of fear, fear of being hurt, fear of missing God, even fear of just being in the wrong relationship. But see, that's how I know that you're someone special. When we started to talk and learn about each other, there was no fear in sharing my emotions, there was no fear of wearing my heart on my sleeve. Your perfect love, which is the love that God shows toward us, drove all my fear away." I wanted to cry, he made me feel so special, like how I was supposed to be treated.

"Oh James, you are so sweet." He grabbed my hand. The bracelet dangled between us.

"That's why I want to know if you would consider being my girlfriend. I care about you too much to not have you on my arm and be committed to giving you everything you need."

My mouth dropped open as I listened to his heartfelt words. My stomach flipped and my heart wanted to jump out of my chest. This was the most romantic thing anyone ever did for me.

"Yes, James." I hugged him again and turned around to see Monique and Kristen sitting at a table, clearly watching the whole thing.

"Did they know about this?" I asked him.

"Yeah, Monique went with me to pick out the bracelet and Kristen was just there, I guess.

We sat and talked for a while about the rest of our day, our classes, and finally about our decision, and then the bell rang.

"Alright Babe, I'll see you after school; I can take you home today."

"Alright, I'll meet you at your locker." I walked away admiring my bracelet and thinking about everything he said. "See God, your so good to me. I knew he was gonna be my boyfriend." I chuckled to myself walking down the hallway. After that altercation we had a few months back, we really straightened our act up. Especially me. I knew that if was going to be with him, I had to do right by him. My mom was right. Today was a good day.

CHAPTER 17

As I walked in the door with a big grin on my face, the phone rang.
"Hello," I said.

"Hey Kiva, it's Jessica. Can I speak to Justin?" I looked at the phone and tried not to roll my eyes.

"This is who?"

"Jessica." I hung up the phone and layed back in my bed. I was protecting my brother. But I guess I had to be nice to the girl; that would be more Christ like.

The phone rang again. I knew that I had to explain to her why I hung up, just in case she thought it was an accident.

"Hello," I said again.

"Hey Kiva, what happened?"

"Well, Jessica I hung up because I really don't like what's going on between you and my brother, but I have to let him work out his own issues and problems. But just for future reference, don't mess him over, 'cause you will have me to deal with."

"Just to be clear, Akiva, whatever happens between me and your brother has nothing at all to do with you. Besides, you know nothing about our relationship and you have no place to say anything, now can you please put my man on the phone." She wasn't getting an argument out of me; she could save it for one of her little chicken-headed friends on the street.

"Well, Jessica, as far as I'm concerned, whatever happens to my brother has a lot to do with me, and I am sad you feel that way, but I'm not gonna sit here and debate with you. Jessica, don't play with my brother's emotions. He really likes you, and if you hurt him, like I think you will, we are gonna have some problems."

"Whatever Kiva, just put Justin on the phone." I put the phone down and yelled for him down the stairs.

"Justin! Your girlfriend is on the phone!"

"Tell her I'll call her back in like fifteen minutes."

"Not a problem," I picked up the phone, let her know and quickly hung it up.

"Now why you gotta be like that Sis, you know you ain't right." He walked in my room and slouched down in my rocking chair.

"Justin, I'm your big sister, okay, I'm trying to warn you about her." He rolled his eyes.

"A.J. Dang, I love her, you know?"

"Justin, what do you love about her?" He looked at his shoes and thought about it real hard.

"Her smile, the way she hugs me, the way she makes me feel. She always tellin' me how good I look and how smart I am. When we spend time together, she always shows me love. She can never get enough of me, you know, and she's so smart."

"Justin, you just named every emotion in the book. You need to know what type of person she is, things like does she fear God, does she have goals and dreams, does she know the purpose of her life, does she plan on being a whoremonger forever, or just dressing like one? Those type of questions."

He gave me a horrible stare and then ignored my statement.

"I understand, and I know all that. But Jessica is special to me, so now all I can do is love her for her, and not what she's supposed to do in her life."

"You know that's not what I meant, but love is not going to pay the bills or keep a marriage alive, only God can do that, and if he's not first, how do you expect you guys to be of one accord? If you followin' your heart, you followin' the wrong thing, brotha."

"How you gonna tell me not to follow my heart?" he asked. I got up and pulled out my Bible from the dresser drawer and flipped through it while he came and sat on my bed.

"Look, Jeremiah 17:9-10 says, '*The heart is deceitful above all things, and desperately wicked: who can know it?*' Basically what this is saying is, you can't listen to your heart, you have to follow the word of God. Look at this verse, Matthew 12:34 and down a little, *'For out of the overflow of the heart, the mouth speaks.'* Pastor Grayson talked about this Sunday. Our minds have to be renewed in the word of God, and then the decisions we make will be based on that. My heart is going to follow my emotions, but my mind renewed in Christ will follow the word."

Justin looked at me as if he didn't understand. "What are you talking about, and what does this have to do with me and Jessica?"

"Well, for one you must be in a place with God where your emotions won't get tied up in anyone that you haven't prayed about or know is sup-posed to be a positive part of your life, because all the time you spend with that person is less time with God. Two, as far as Jessica is concerned, if you two don't have the same motives or beliefs, you won't be happy, and God won't be able to help if he's not wanted in the relationship.

"Three, that last verse means that if you get your heart right with God, things will start to produce in your life that will bring you closer to God, and as long as you have him as head of your life, he will put everything else in order. I'm not saying God is looking for a perfect person, because we can't be that, but he's looking for a perfect heart and in order for us to attain that, we must stay in his presence and out of the presence of evil-doers; we must follow his words, and be obedient to him."

"Where did you learn all that stuff from, 'cause we don't get this deep in teen Sunday school," Justin said with a smile.

"Well, if you read your word from time to time and not just on Sunday and Wednesday, maybe you would know some of this stuff." I pulled his ear. Justin came and sat on my bed and kicked off his shoes.

"So how will I know if she's the one I'm supposed to be with?" he asked.

"You have to pray about it, you just can't think that she's the one just because you love her." I pulled my hair back into a ponytail and Justin got a glimpse of my new bracelet.

"Who gave you that?"

"James gave it to me, nosy; why you so worried?" I said, admiring my bracelet.

"I John 4:18; what does that verse say?"

"It talks about perfect love casting out all fear." Justin sat there for a while and then grabbed my arm and pulled it gently.

"Aww, that is so sweet girl, he love you!" I laughed and hit him with a pillow.

"Whateva, Sucka."

"But you know what, though, James is cool.

"Yeah," I said, getting up and walking to my closet. "He is a pretty cool guy." I grabbed a sweater and sat back down on the bed.

Our parents walked in as we were talking. My mom sat down in the chair, and my dad stood in front of the dresser.

"Wassup, Mom and Dad?" I asked

"We just wanted to come in and say goodnight, that's all." My mom smiled and gave my brother a hug and me a kiss on the cheek.

"Alright goodnight." I said, but my dad was still standing.

"Kiva, let me talk to you in private."

I was trying to think, what did I do?

"Dad, I'm about to go to sleep. I have school tomorrow."

He sat on my bed and rubbed my back. "Alright, Sweetie. Do you know what kind of calling you have on your life?" He looked straight into my eyes. All of a sudden, I got nervous.

"I know that I am called to the ministry, but in what capacity, I don't know." I looked at the wall, wondering what my father was going to say.

"Akiva, you have big things ahead of you. God was telling me last night that I have watched you grow from a young lady to an adult, and in that time you have been diligent. You haven't been perfect but you always loved him with your whole heart. Akiva, God has something in store for you that is great, eye has not seen nor ear has heard girl, you betta walk into what God has. But listen to me on this one thing; stay focused on three things; God and his word, your goals for your life, and your family. These three things are going to be the building blocks for what you are called to do."

"Alright, Daddy." He gave me hug and a kiss on the forehead, and walked out. God is so good, and I am so blessed to have a family like them. Even though they get on my nerves sometimes, God has really shown me how to appreciate their uniqueness and love them for who they are. I wrapped my hair up and put on my nightgown. I slipped under the warm covers and let out a sigh. My bed felt so good. Just as I was about to grab the phone to call James, my brother walked in again.

"What do you want and why are you in my closet?"

"So do you have my sweater that's light blue and pink? I saw you eyeing it one day, and I can't find it in my closet or in my drawers." I rolled my eyes and got out of the bed.

"Here," I said, pulling it out of the back of my closet. It was on a hook behind all of my clothes so that if he came in here looking, I would know. He laughed and threw the sweater over his shoulder.

"Bye, Justin," I said as he walked out the door. He turned around and leaned back on the door.

"You know what, A.J.?"

"What?"

"All this evening, you threw scriptures at me, and they all had a place in my life to help me grow. I feel like I should have known at least half the stuff that you were talking about. I felt kind of left out."

"Well, God doesn't want you to feel left out, but he also can't force you to open your Bible; that's your decision."

"What if Jessica isn't the one I'm supposed to be with? What if I never find anyone like her? She is that deal, man. She was a one-of-a-kind woman."

"Justin, God is the creator of everything, and just how he created Jessica, he can create someone else to be your mate, but you need to first focus on Christ and your relationship with him. Then and only then will he give you your mate." He nodded and walked out of the room. I liked being an older sister, but now it was time to be a girlfriend.

CHAPTER 18

Hello, may I speak to James please?"

"Yup, hold on one second Dear."

"Hello," James answered the phone sounding tired.

"Hey Baby, I just wanted to call and say goodnight. I hope I didn't wake you."

I rolled over in the bed getting more comfortable.

"Kiva, I love to hear your voice, you can call me anytime, Baby." I got all warm inside.

"So how was the rest of your day?" he asked.

"It was good, when I think about my whole senior year James, I just really think about how much I've grown you know."

"Mhm."

"Between friendships, relationships, church, and school, God has just really been doing a lot in my life." He didn't sound like he was interested in what I was saying.

"Hello,"

"I'm here Kiva. Can I tell you something?"

"Yeah."

"I have known you for four years, I even remember the first time we met our freshman year. I have always been attracted to everything about you, and even in the mistakes you made with guys and stuff, I knew that you were still someone trying to do right. Akiva, I truly in my heart believe you are going to be my wife, and I love you with all my heart. We have only been dating for a short time, but there is no doubt in my mind that we can get through anything together. I have seen your growth, and

I want to grow with you Babe." I wanted to cry. He was the sweetest guy in the world.

"Wow, James, I knew you loved me; but your wife one day? That's a big thing. What made you tell me all this tonight?" There was a pause. I wasn't sure if I should be nervous or excited.

"Well, after much prayer and research, I decided what college I'm going to." We had been talking about going to the same school, I wanted to go to Oakland and do social work, and he could go there and do their law program. We had both been accepted, seen the campus, and had pretty much decided that's where we were headed, until he got a letter in the mail from Northwestern in Illinois that he got a scholarship. He was excited, and was thinking that Northwestern may be a good place to go. I didn't want to stop him from following his dreams, but I wanted him to be with me, so I just stayed quiet about it. I guess he had finally decided whether he was going to take the four hour hike from Detroit to Chicago, or stay here with me.

"So where did you decide Baby?" I asked innocently. I was hoping it was Oakland, please say Oakland!

"Baby, I'm going to Columbia in New York."

CHAPTER 19

The last basketball game of the season was always the best. *"Dribble it (clap clap), pass it (clap clap), we want a basket!"* The cheerleaders rooted for the boys as Nate went up for a lay up. It rolled around the net and went in. Everyone in the stands jumped up, and the cheerleaders did toe touches to show their approval.

Our school really came together when it had to do with sports. I sat back on my bench and looked across the gym. On our side were students with either green or white Comm. Tech paraphernalia or their cutest outfit on. Most of the girls had on their leather jackets, tight jeans, and boots, and the guys had on big leather jackets with fur around the hood, baggy jeans, and Timberlands.

Since the game was at 5:00 p.m., I told Ananda to meet me at my school and then she could come over after and we could chill at my house until it was time for her to go home. It was 5:15 and I was still waiting. I sat there looking at the cheerleading team, glad I never joined. Shayla, James ex-girlfriend, was the captain, and she was clearly standing in the need of prayer. Since the cheerleaders practiced the same time as the basketball team, James said he had to watch out for her because she would always be in his face. I told him it's because we're together now, and she doesn't like that. She looked up in the bleachers at me, rolled her eyes and screamed "Go, James, go!" People are so immature these days. My phone rang; it was Ananda.

"Hey girl, where you at?" I asked.

"I'm at the door; it's a line out here. But girl, guess who's about four people in front of me?"

"Who?"

"Alex." My mouth dropped. He had called me a couple times after our date, and I had tried to avoid him as much as possible. Hopefully, he would act like he didn't know me.

"I doubt if he will say anything to me," I said, hoping he wouldn't.

"I don't know; he wit your girls and you know they like to keep mess up."

"Who?"

"Shawny and Natalie." I knew Shawny was just tryin' to start some drama. She had no life, but I wasn't gonna let her get to me. I was here to support James and have a good time.

"How many of them are there?"

"It looks like the two girls, Alex, and two of his boys."

"But can they let them in if they don't have high school ID?"

"Girl, please, they looking for that little measly three dollars from them; they don't care." I just knew that there might be some unwanted drama tonight.

"I see them walking in. Good, they're sittin' on the other side."

"Alright, I'll be there in a minute." I looked at James to see if he saw them, and by this time he was on the bench. He wiped his face and looked at all five of them walk in and sit down. Something was goin' on, and he knew it too.

Ananda came in a couple minutes later, struttin' her stuff. She walked past the cheerleaders, and Shayla looked at her like she knew her. Ananda had on the cutest outfit, and the baddest heels I had seen in a long time. They matched her jacket exactly. I was always glad she was my best friend. Not only did she know how to take care of the outside, she was one of the most beautiful people on the inside. I stood up so she could see me.

"Hey girl!" she yelled, slowly walking up the bleachers. We hugged and sat back down.

"James is on the bench now, but when Shawny and 'dem walked in, he looked like he knew who they were."

"James is cute," she commented, hitting me on the shoulder.

"Thanks, girl; I try." We laughed as she took off her jacket and I watched the little group from afar.

"That's Shayla, James' ex-girlfriend," I said, looking towards the cheerleaders.

"You mean that little girl that grimmed me? She looked like I did something to her."

"You did; you came in here lookin' like a diva. She ain't like that, Girl!" We laughed as we got settled on the hard benches.

After awhile, we decided to go grab a hot dog and walk around while the game was going on. By the time we came back, the game was almost over and James was back in.

"Alright James, do ya thing boy!" I yelled. Ananda rolled her eyes and pulled my arm back down.

"Girl, you are so ghetto."

"Whatever, Girl, it's hatas all around." Finally, the buzzer went off and the game was over. We waited in the bleachers while everyone else cleared out. While Ananda and I were talking, I looked over to the other side of the bench and I saw the five sitting over there trying to watch Ananda and me. I guess they thought we were going to leave, but I had to see my James, and I was not having any drama tonight, hopefully.

Five minutes later, Alonzo, Nate, and James came out of the locker room. James looked over to the other side of the bleachers, saw them, and walked in my direction.

"Hey Baby, you played a good game," I said, standing up and giving him a hug.

He smiled and put his bag down. "Thanks, Sweetheart. Is this your friend?" He looked at Ananda.

"Yes, this is my best friend, Ananda. Ananda, this is James." He shook her hand and sat down on the bleacher right below me.

"Did you enjoy the game?" he asked.

"Yeah, it was cool," Ananda said.

"I figured that, seeing y'all left for half the game to get something to eat. I thought y'all went out to eat as long as y'all was gone." We all laughed as he laid his head back on my leg. I put my legs to the side so they wouldn't be open and his head ended up on my thigh. As soon as he closed his eyes and wiped his forehead, a loud voice came from the other side of the gym.

"For real, Kiva, it's like that!" We all looked to the other side of the gym where Alex and his boys were sitting.

My heart dropped.

"Who is that?" Alonzo asked.

"I don't know, but I'm about to find out." James stood up, I looked at Ananda with big wide eyes, and her mouth dropped as Alex started to walk across the gym floor.

"Kiva, what up Boo, you don't know how to return phone calls?" He and his boy were still walking towards us and I was frozen.

"Kiva, do you know him?" James asked. I didn't know how to respond.

"Yeah she knows me clown, oh, and you must be old dude she was talkin' about." He smirked at him, and winked at me.

By this time, I had gained some of my composure, but before I could say anything, Ananda jumped in.

"Alex, Kiva don't want you, and don't try to act like y'all got something going on, 'cause y'all don't."

Alex licked his lips and looked at me with those beautiful eyes.

"Kiva, you wanna hang tonight?" He asked with so much confidence, like he just knew I was gonna say yes. Why was this happening to me?

"Alex, I have avoided your phone calls for a reason, why would you try to play me like this? You know ain't nothin' going on with us, and I ain't leavin' here with you." I said it in my most confident voice I could muster up.

"You heard her, man, she don't want nothin' to do wit you." James chimed in.

"Man wasn't nobody talkin' to you!" Alex walked up on James, and James posted up tough. Alonzo and Nate were right behind him, and I could see at that moment, that it wasn't about me anymore, but manly pride.

"James, it's not worth it dude, you don't even know this fool man, he just tryin' to start some mess." Nate got some sense and stepped in between Alex and James, pushing James back.

"Yeah you betta get ya boy to hold ya back, 'cause I'll put you up in the hospital tonight."

"Alex motioned to his friend to leave and they walked out chuckling.

"Kiva," He yelled my name one last time.

"Im'ma see you at church Boo." He kept laughing and walking. I can't believe this just happened.

Ananda shook her head. James grabbed his bag and started walking toward the gym entrance. He looked upset and I could understand why.

"Ananda, I just want to go home. I really don't feel like going out to eat or anything."

"You sure?"

"Yeah, I'm sure." We walked to the car in silence and just as I was about to open the door to Ananda's car, James sped off.

"He didn't even say bye."

"Give him a minute to cool off; call him tonight." We got in the car and drove to my house. As I sat in the passenger seat, I pushed the seat back and put my arms above my head. I couldn't believe Alex's stunt, what was he trying to prove?

I shook my head and looked out the window. I could see small snowflakes flying through the air, landing on the cement and joining with the rest of the flakes to make one big pile of snow. The sidewalks were already covered, and I couldn't even see the names of the streets. As we got closer to my house, the wind started blowing more and more snow. What was he thinking? It wasn't like he didn't know what was going on? I told him about Alex, so he shouldn't be that mad, maybe after a few days he would forgive me and everything would be back to normal? That sure was my prayer.

CHAPTER 20

CALLED OUT

ey everybody!" I yelled, taking off my shoes. We walked through the house and no one seemed to be there, so we went up to my room.

"Where is everybody?" Ananda asked.

"They're probably all in the basement watching a movie." She knocked on my brother's door.

"What?"

"Dang, boy, I just wanted to say hi. How you doin'?" Ananda asked pleasantly.

"I'm fine, but busy. Can I talk to you another day?"

"Alright, bye. I ju—" Before she could get her words out, he slammed the door in her face. I chuckled as she walked back feeling kind of awkward. "Dang, what did I do to him?"

"Nothin' Girl; you know him and Jessica been going through their ups and downs lately." A couple seconds later he peeked his head in my door with the same look he gave Ananda.

"Hey, Mom is in the basement watching TV and Dad is at church with Pastor Grayson."

I looked back at him and rolled my eyes.

"Justin, who else would he be at the church with? Alright thanks." He sighed, walked back out, and slammed his door. Ananda took off her jacket and threw it on the rocker as I began to wrap my hair.

"Can you get in the door first before you start wrapping your hair?"

"I'm sorry; I can't put my hair in a ponytail and just wrap it before I take a shower. My hair has to be trained. I can't give it a chance to do it's own thang." We laughed and turned on the television. I went downstairs to go pop some popcorn and the doorbell rang.

"That's probably Kristen," I said to myself. I pranced to the door, looked out the peephole and let her in. She walked in the door wearing boots and a big black coat and the saddest look I had ever seen on her face.

"What's wrong, Kris? What happened?" I asked, taking her coat and putting it in the closet.

"Kiva, man, I fell."

"Did you hurt yourself?" I looked for a scrape.

"No, Kiva."

"Then what?"

"Kiva, me and Oliver did it last night. Man, it's so hard to let that go. I've been tryin', it's just that I love being around him, and I'm so used to being with him. I knew that if I stayed at my house, he would have ended up coming over." Wow. I was shocked that she opened up to me like that.

"Well, Kris, you've been having sex for awhile, so I know it's probably hard to stop, but you have repented and all of that is forgiven."

"I know that, Kiva, but I need something more than that, something to encourage me, show me my faults, and help me get right."

She wanted me to bring out the big guns. I didn't really know that many scriptures on sex 'cause I didn't plan on having any, but I knew the Lord would show me what to say.

"Look at this verse, 1 Corinthians 6:9: *'Do you not know that the wicked will not inherit the kingdom of God? Do not be deceived; Neither the sexually immoral nor idolators nor adulterers nor male prostitutes nor homosexual offenders. . .* Now go down and look at this verse, 1 Corinthians 13, go down a little:"

> *"The body is not meant for sexual immortality, but for the Lord, and the Lord for the body, by his power God raised the Lord from the dead, and he will raise us also. Do you not know that your bodies are members of Christ himself? Shall I then take the members of Christ and unite them with a prostitute? Never! Do you not know that he who unites himself with a prostitute is one with her in body? For it is said, The two will become one flesh, but he who unites himself with the Lord is one with him in spirit."*

We sat there for a couple more minutes just talking about how important it is to reverence God in your body, because it's always going to be a fight.

"That's why the word says greater is he in me, then he that is of the world, because your flesh may want to have sex, but your spirit should be stronger and be able to tell your flesh no. Where you are weak, God makes his strength perfect."

"That's cool and all, but what about when it's just me and him and my flesh gets weak?"

"Well for one, you shouldn't put yourself in positions where that could happen. That's called using wisdom, and believe me, God will add his wisdom to you if you just ask for it, but I thought we were leaving Oliver alone anyway?" I said putting the Bible back up.

"Yeah, I'm trying, but sometimes I just get lonely."

I grabbed the Bible again. "Kristen, when you get lonely you can't go to a man because his love is conditional, but you can go to Jesus and he will give you love with no strings attached. You have to understand he made you, so he knows what makes you happy, he knows how to please you and be your best friend. You have to grow a closer relationship with him. Before you can commit to a man, you have to commit to God whole-heartedly. How can you love a man unconditionally through the good times and bad, when he cheats on you, when he lies, and when he breaks your heart, but you can't love your God who sent his only son to die for you, never does anything to harm you, and has only your best intentions at hand, you can't beat that."

She sat back on the couch, thinking.

"We don't have to worry about what we did in the past, just move forward and walk into what God has for us. He forgot about it, and we should too. Look at this verse 1 John 4:7-10:

> "Dear friends, let us love one another, for love comes from God. Everyone who loves has been born of God and knows God. Whoever does not love does not know God, because God is love, this is how God showed his love among us: He sent his one and only son into the world that we might live through him. Not that we loved God, but that he loved us and sent his son as an atoning sacrifice for our sins."

She grabbed the Bible and read the verse again. I scooted closer to her and put my arm around her.

"God understands, and he has your back, but you have to let him take control and overcome the flesh." She put her head on my shoulder and started to cry. I rubbed her back and tried to console her.

The flesh is a killer. It will have you out here fightin' people because of anger, smoking even though you don't like it, drinkin' because your friends are, or making you depressed. That's why we have to continually fight it, and follow God's word so that we stay in his will. I don't think people understand when our pastors or Sunday school teachers say that this is a way of life, but it is. The Bible tells us how to live our lives every day, and we don't because it's not taught to us, or we don't know where to start.

As the tears rolled, I started to pray for strength in her life to be able to overcome the flesh. She wiped her tears and stood up.

"A.J., you are the closest person to me; my mother is hardly there, I don't have a boyfriend, and I don't talk to people in school. And even though I treated you like crap sometimes, you were still there for me. Thank you."

"Kristen, he's going to add restoration to your life. You and your mom will grow closer, but you have to pray about it and seek God and read the word about what to do."

Just as Kristen was about to speak, Ananda came downstairs into the kitchen.

"Hey A.J., I was lookin' for some... oh, hey Kristen." Ananda said nonchalantly.

"Hey Ananda, how are you doing?"

Ananda leaned up against the door and folded her arms. "I'm well."

I knew that Ananda and Kristen didn't really get along, but as long as I was here, there was gonna be no drama. I was sick and tired of it, and if we had to read the Bible all night to keep the peace, so be it.

"We were just talking about some things. Did you need something?"

"Um, I was looking for the tape 'cause one of your posters fell, but that's cool. Can we watch a movie or something?"

"Yeah, we should order a pizza and rent some movies," Kristen said in mild excitement.

"Excuse me, we have school tomorrow, or did you guys forget that?"

"Have you looked at the news? We ain't goin' nowhere no time soon."

Justin said, walking down the stairs. I turned on the news and saw the weatherman standing in the blizzard.

"Tonight we will have strong winds and blowing snow. Some schools have already announced a no school warning." Ananda and Kristen jumped up and down as the names of our schools scrolled across the screen.

Even Eastern Michigan University was closing. "Yes, maybe I can spend some time with Jeff tomorrow!" Ananda went upstairs to grab her phone.

But Justin's school wasn't listed. "Man, that's straight up shady; I still gotta go to school tomorrow!" Kristen and I laughed quietly as he sauntered back up the stairs. Five minutes later my dad walked in, covered in snow.

"Hey Kiva Baby, hey Kristen. Is that Ananda's car parked in the back?" Dad asked as he took off his boots.

"Yeah, it was snowing really bad so she decided to just stay here for the night, which worked out because we don't have school tomorrow!" I hugged him with excitement. He put his head back and rolled his eyes. "Oh Lord Jesus, help us all!" Kristen laughed and I hugged my father even closer.

"Well, your mother and I still have to go to work, so I expect you guys to be on your best behavior." He put his finger on my forehead as I agreed to his instructions. He walked around me and opened the refrigerator as Mom came upstairs to clean up the kitchen.

"Mom, tomorrow night, can you make me a cheesecake?" I asked, trying to sound innocent.

She looked back at me and turned around. "Yes, child, now go with your friends before I change my mind."

I ran upstairs and found that Justin was in my room with Kristen and Ananda throwing pillows at them. When I walked in, he threw a pillow right at my face without looking back. I charged right at him and knocked him to the floor.

"Kids, look, it's late and I am not tryin' to hear y'all all night. Y'all betta get right, 'cause y'all not too old to get whipped!" Dad yelled from the bathroom. We all laughed silently and decided to go to the basement and watch a movie.

"I'm 'bout to go to bed, 'cause I got school tomorrow." Justin pulled up his baggy jeans and walked to the kitchen.

"Boy, that ain't your bedroom," I said, walking down the stairs.

"I know, but I'm getting hungry. Im'ma grab a sandwich or somethin'."

We all walked downstairs and fell onto the couch, excited that there was no school. We didn't know what to do, but we knew we were staying up all night.

"I know, let's play on some people's phones!" Kristen said. Ananda and I looked at each other and smiled. Kristen ran for the house phone and Ananda and I searched through our cell phones to find someone to call.

"Let's call Alex, I'll bet that'll be funny." Kristen grabbed my phone. She picked up the house phone, pressed *67, and began to dial his number. After three rings, he picked up.

"Hello."

"Wassup, man? This Rod," Kristen said in the deepest voice she could muster.

"Rod? I don't know no Rod."

"Alex, it's Rod. I used to stay off Greenfield and Puritan on Robson; we went to Cerveny Middle School together." Alex started to act like he knew who he was, and I looked at Ananda, trying not to laugh.

"Oh wassup, man, how you been." Alex played it off like he knew him.

"I'm cool man, but it's some dudes on my block; they wanna get at you, dude."

"What they wanna get at me for?" Alex asked sounding confused.

"Dawg, one of 'em said you used to mess with they girl, and the other one said you beat him down a while ago."

"What was they names?" he asked.

"Man, I don't even want to get into all that. But I let 'em know that you was my boy, and I wasn't playin' that. They calmed down after that." By this time Ananda and I were trying not to laugh; she was covering my mouth and hers to keep from messing up the joke.

"Good lookin' out, man, they yo boys or somethin'?"

"Naw, Al, I just know 'em cause they stay around here. But look, though, let me get your address." Our mouths dropped. If Alex was dumb enough to give his address, then I was totally through.

"What you need my address for? You tight."

"Well, I was just gonna run through real quick, nothing' deep." Kristen was trying to hold back her laughter and talk at the same time.

"Naw, dawg, you straight; I ain't tryin to hear all that." We could tell that Alex knew something was up by then.

"Alright man, well. I'll holla. Maybe next time we can chill out, you know."

"Yeah man, and don't give your boys my number, aiight?" Alex sounded upset.

"Naw man, I wouldn't do nuthin' like that; you my boy."

"Aiight then."

"Aiight, I'll holla." She hung up the phone and all three of us burst into laughter.

"I cannot believe you did that! I'm surprised he answered the phone," Ananda said.

"Girl, how did you know all that information about him?" I asked.

"Because Oliver used to talk about how they knew this guy named Rod who always was in the middle of everything. He was always instigating everybody's mess, so I just played that role."

"You were so funny; let's do another one."

CHAPTER 21

It was cold. After one day out of school, we came back to a freezing cold building. They wouldn't let us wear our coats in school, but thank God I had brought a sweater to school and had another one in my locker.

"Students, today we are going to fill out some college applications and learn about the various majors you can take." Mr. Walsh started to pass out applications down the rows. It seemed kind of late to me though. I had filled out my applications in November and it was late January now. So far, I had gotten accepted to University of Michigan Ann Arbor, Central State, Eastern Michigan University, and Oakland University. Oakland was probably where I was gonna end up though. I loved their campus.

James walked in the class late looking drab. As he walked past, I hit him on the leg and he just turned around and looked. No facial expression or anything. I hadn't talked to him since the basketball game, but I thought he would be over it by now.

"Ok students, we're gonna break off into groups and look at the applications. How many students in here are already accepted to universities?" Over half the class raised their hands. Our teacher looked shocked and amazed. The biggest myth about Detroit Public Schools is that we never learned anything, but when you go to schools like Comm. Tech, Renaissance, Communication and Media Arts High School, Crockett, and all those other schools of choice, over half of those students are going to a college. I decided to join the group with James, Alonzo, Eric, and Kristen—biggest mistake I've ever made. I got my stuff out of my seat. As I walked over, James reluctantly cleared out the seat next to him and pulled it closer to his stuff. At least he wasn't as mad as before.

"Wassup, dawg, how is life treatin' ya?" Eric asked while giving pound to Alonzo and James.

"Man, life is good fa sho." Alonzo replied.

"I hear that," James chimed in.

"Man, did you see that game last night? The Lakers ain't playin no games out here."

"Here we go," I whispered in Kristen's ear. She laughed as all the boys started talking at the same time about the game and the players. A couple minutes later, Mr. Walsh was standing over us.

"Excuse me, Ladies and Gentlemen, we should be talking about school, not basketball games." he pushed up his glasses and handed us each two applications.

"Mr. W, I already filled out applications and I know where I'm going in the fall." Eric was a gossip, but he was always on his schoolwork. Mr. Walsh stood there glaring at Eric as if he had just cussed at him, straightened up his tie, and leaned on my desk.

"Well, Mr. Smith, where are you going in the fall?" He had an attitude and I think all of us wondered why.

"I'm going to Michigan State. My mom and dad went there, my brother goes there and my aunt teaches there. I got my acceptance letter last week and Im'ma be playing ball." Mr. Walsh looked embarrassed. It wasn't our fault he was late doing the application process. We were on our job, thanks to our high school counselor, Mrs. Holt. She was the best counselor; everybody wanted her, but she only had ninth and twelfth graders this year.

"Alright students, since most of you have already filled out applications, the ones who haven't, go to that side of the room and we can work on them. If you have, stay on this side and talk quietly for the remainder of the period."

We all sat there shocked that he didn't give us a reading assignment, but we were cool with it anyway.

"I don't know why he would have us do this in homeroom anyway; everybody in here isn't a senior," Alonzo said.

"Right, what's the purpose of me filling out an application when I have three more years to go," Kristen added.

"Well, you know him and Ms. Holt don't get along, so she probably just wants to do something to make her mad," I replied. Everybody smacked their teeth and rolled their eyes at how stupid their beef was.

"Well, excuse me," I said, rolling my eyes and facing toward James.

"Wassup, Sweetie?" I asked, smiling.

"Nothin' much." He said plainly.

"So you forgive me?" I batted my eyes.

"Kiva, I'm not about to talk to you about this right now."

I looked over and the whole group was all in our conversation.

Eric looked at Kristen and then looked at James.

"Man just forgive her Dude, you know it was probably your fault anyway." Everybody at the table started laughing except for James and I.

"Eric, stay out of it man, you don't know what's going on." James said with a serious face.

"C'mon man, I'm just joking around." He cracked a smile, and then started laughing again.

I looked at James and motioned for him to come into the hallway with me.

"Look James, I'm so sorry that happened the other night, you know I don't talk to him anymore and that I'm all about you. He was just trying to push your buttons. I don't want to lose you over no crap like that. I'm sorry."

He was staring at the floor with his hands in his pockets shaking his head and smirking.

"You just don't get it Kiva, that was embarrassing! Old Dude tried to fight me. What if I would have swung on him or him on me? I'm not for the drama Kiva."

I looked at him confused.

"But James, you know that I didn't put him up to that. I can't control what basketball game he attends, or how he acts toward you. I apologized, and I don't know what else you want me to do. I tried to give you your space, but it seems like you want to be upset with me." I was almost in tears by this time and I was trying not to cry in the middle of the hallway.

"Look Kiva, I forgive you, and I love you. I don't blame you for what happened, just give me some space okay?" This was so stupid to me, but if I wanted to be with him, this was my choice.

"Alright, James, Whatever you want."

CHAPTER 22

CALLED OUT

I couldn't believe how cold it was outside. My mom wasn't feeling well, so my dad had to drop us off at school, which meant that I had to leave early. Daddy dropped me off in front of the school, and I walked in feeling pretty good.

I walked to my locker and threw my coat in. I pulled out the books that I didn't need and threw them in my locker. As I put my messenger bag over my shoulder and closed my locker, I turned around to Shawny, Natalie, and two other girls on the cheerleading team. I leaned back on my locker calmly and smiled.

"Hey Kiva, how you doin'?" Natalie asked with a smirk on her face.

"I'm good; how about yourself?" I kept smiling. They weren't gonna kill my joy.

"I bet you are. It's sad that people talk about they saved and then you find out their livin' another life."

I stood up straight and asked, "Natalie, what are you talking about?"

"I heard you and that boy Alex was gettin' y'all freak on. Girl, I didn't know you liked those type of dudes? Hope it didn't blow up in your face too much at the basketball game" I smacked my lips and leaned back on the locker.

"I ain't did nothing with Alex, and you know it, why are you all in my business anyway?"

"Oh I'm just looking out for my friend James, you know we go way back." Natalie and Shawny burst into laughter and at that moment, I wanted to bust her jaw. I looked Shawny dead in her eyes.

"Shawny, I don't know what your problem is, but you need help. Every other week, you tryin' to cause drama in somebody's life. My man and his

171

business is none of yours, and for the record, stay out of mine, too, James doesn't like nosy girls." I rolled my eyes and walked away.

"Yeah, we'll see when you're here at Oakland and he is in New York with me. Won't take him that long to forget about you then. Oh yeah, I didn't tell you I got accepted to NYU, did I?" I continued to walk toward my classroom as tears welled up in my eyes. Why, every week, was there drama, Lord? What happened to my prayer? Why didn't it get answered? I was tired of Shawny, I was tired of Comm. Tech, and I was definitely tired of always being good. When, all of a sudden, did her interest for James turn into "Hate on Akiva" mission? I walked into the classroom trying to hold my tears back when Eric walked up to me.

"What's going on A.J.? You straight?" I really didn't want to talk to anybody, especially nosy Eric. I wiped my tears on my sleeve and sat up with a smile on my face.

"I'm cool Eric, have you seen James?"

"Oh, he's not coming to school today. Remember when Ms. Holt said she was going to take the students with the 50 highest G.P.A's to Bowling Green? That was today, so he won't be back until fourth hour." Dang, when I really needed someone to talk to, he wasn't there.

A couple minutes later, Kristen walked in the room angry. Her sleeves were rolled up and her face was red. She grabbed a desk near me, threw her books down on the floor, and slouched in her seat.

"Kiva, have you seen Shawny this morning?" I could tell she was trying to be calm, but it wasn't working.

"Yeah, her and Natalie came in my face talkin' about all that stuff that happened with Alex."

"Well, apparently, she saw Oliver in the mall the other day, and she was bragging about how she was all up on him, and how he asked for her number. If I see her, Kiva, you might have to hold me back, 'cause Im'ma sock her. I ain't afraid of her sorry—"

"Kristen, calm down, okay? Look, you don't want Oliver, so let her have him, if it's even true. Don't let her get under your skin Kristen, she isn't worth it." I rubbed her back and she sat there with the meanest look on her face. I would hate to be on Kristen's bad side.

The bell rang and we walked out, wondering what the rest of the day would bring. I walked to my locker, opened it, and laid my head on the door.

"Lord, I know you won't put more on me than I can bear, so I'm trusting that you will take care of my enemies. Forgive them, Father, and show them that they messed with the wrong girl. I'm a King's kid, and I am not to be played with. If I have made any mistakes, please forgive me. I'm just gonna keep my mouth shut 'cause that just seems like the holiest thing to do right now. I love you. In Jesus' name I pray, Amen."

I was okay now. Hopefully, with God's help, I could make it through the rest of the day.

The fourth hour bell rang, and I sat in my classroom waiting for my knight in shining armor to walk through the door. Monique walked in and sat behind me. Just as I thought she was going to do something stupid, she passed me a note. It read:

> Dear A.J.,
>   I'm sorry I have been a jerk to you. I guess I was
> jealous because it seemed like you and James were
> doing so well, and I didn't have anybody. I'm sorry,
> and I hope you accept my apology.
>
> Love,
> Monique

I smiled and wrote her back:

> Monique,
>   Girl, you know I accept your apology. You my girl,
> and I missed you. I was Hoping you were gonna come
> back to your senses!
>
> A.J

As soon as I gave the note back to Monique, James walked in the door. He looked so good. He had on khaki pants and a cream and khaki colored top with beige shoes and a pencil behind his ear. He sat in the seat in front of me and quickly wrote me a note and passed it to me.

Hey Kiva,
  I already heard about what happened this morning. Don't worry about it. Im'ma talk to Shawny next
hour and Im'ma settle this. I'm sorry for taking my
anger out on you, I shouldn't have done that. I know
you only want to be with me. I trust you, and will work
on not doing that again.

Are you okay?

James

See, that's why he was my man! He knew me, and he knew that I would
never do anything like that. I smiled and wrote him a letter back.

I'm cool, but Kristen might end up sockin' Shawny in
her mouth by the end of the day. She came up to her
this morning with Natalie talking about Oliver.
  She was a trip.
  And P.S. Thanks for forgiving me. ☺

He read the note and took a deep breath. Today was just not a good day
at Community Tech, and after school was gonna be a trip. I was ready.
  I slammed my locker door and went down to James' locker after I
heard yelling. I just hoped that it didn't get any worse. When I got there,
Shawny was all in his face.
  "Shawny, Im'ma tell you one time to leave my girl alone, I ain't got
time to be dealing with your drama." James was pissed, and I could see
it all in his face.
  "Ain't my fault yo girl out here trickin'. She need to keep her legs closed."
I dropped my books in the middle of the hallway as James turned around
and slammed the locker above her head. She jumped back against the
locker and looked at James in fear. "Shawny, all these games you been
playin', sending me notes in class, calling my house and hanging up, it's
gonna end now." She tried to look as if she was cool but you could see
the nervousness in her face. By this time, I was walking closer to them.
  "Kiva!"

James backed up off the locker and motioned for me to come closer. I ran as quickly as I could.

"Yes,"

"Shawny, apologize!" She pulled herself off the locker, and rolled her eyes at me.

"I ain't apologizin' for sh**."

"Shawny, just apologize so this can be over." James stepped closer to her and she backed up.

"Ok, okay, James dang, back up off me." She folded her arms and looked off to the side.

"Kiva, my bad for havin' my cousin come up here and start some mess, when he told me he knew you, and that y'all hung out, I wanted James to know." She picked up her books and looked at James.

"You happy?"

"One more thing Shawny." James put his arm around me.

"What."

"This is my girl, I love her, so quit wit all the games, I'm done, okay, done."

She rolled her eyes and walked away flipping her hair.

"Wow, James, I'm so glad that is over. Can you believe that?"

"Naw, that was crazy man, yeah she a trip." We walked over, picked up my books, and continued to walk towards my locker.

"So, she was calling your house, and sending you notes in class? You didn't tell me about that."

"Well, that's another story for another day."

"Yeah, whatever James."

CHAPTER 23

Baked chicken, macaroni and cheese, Greek salad, mixed vegetables, rolls and rice pilaf—what's the occasion?" Justin asked as he walked into the kitchen before me.

"Mom. This is a lot of food." I grabbed a celery stick from the refrigerator.

"Where's your father?" she asked, pulling the chicken out of the oven.

"He went upstairs to put his stuff down and change clothes."

Mom put the macaroni and cheese in the oven and pulled off her apron. "You kids go do some homework and come back down in about an hour. Dinner should be ready by then."

I walked upstairs to my room and pulled all the notes out of my purse. I couldn't believe everything that happened today, it was just so much drama, and I felt so responsible. If I would have never given Alex my phone number, this would have never happened. I'm grateful for the experience, because it made James and my relationship stronger, as well as my relationship with God. But wow, what a day. I got on my knees and went under the bed to pull out my shoebox. I pulled off the top and threw those letters in. I had to push the top down to make sure that it stayed on securely. After I slid it back under my bed, I thought about all the letters I had written from ninth grade all the way up to my senior year and why I still had them. I guess I wanted to look back at them when I'm grown.

I went back downstairs, started setting the table for dinner and putting food out. Then my mom asked the question she probably wanted to know for a long time.

179

"So Kiva, where is James going for college? I see you guys are spending more time together?" Mom asked.

"My man, James. I like that boy; he got his head on right." I'm glad Dad liked him, since one day James was gonna be his son-in-law.

"He's going to Columbia, in New York."

"New York?" They seemed surprised.

"Yeah, he said God told him that he needs to be there, and he has a cousin that goes there, so he won't be alone." I tried to keep the tears from falling as I looked out of the window into the backyard. It just hurt so bad to know that he wouldn't be here. I guess I was still takin' it in.

"Don't worry, Baby. Just focus on what you need to do. Let God use you to his glory, and everything will fall into place," said Mom. "Yeah, and you don't need to be worryin' about no husband no way. You ain't even all the way grown, and I ain't ready for payin' for a weddin' or no grandkids." I smacked my lips and my mother smiled and sat on my father's lap. They were so happy. I could tell that through everything, the spark was still there.

"C'mon girl, let's go finish setting this table up for dinner." Mom stood up and grabbed my arm; Dad got up and walked into the living room. He still thought he was exempt from setting the table, but my mama said he was still working on that.

CHAPTER 24

CALLED OUT

R*ring!* The school bell went off and everybody was excited. Our annual Apollo show was always a hit; I just wondered who was getting booed off this year. I went to my locker, grabbed my camera, and threw my books in there. I had decided to be cute today since it was a pretty nice day outside. All the snow had melted and it was about 60 degrees. Michigan weather was the worst, but I wouldn't change it for the world.

"Hey girl, you ready to go?" Monique came up to my locker dressed in light blue pants with a sheer light blue top and light blue boots with a skinny heel.

"Oh, you think you that deal today huh?" I said, pointing at her outfit and smiling.

"Whatever. I'm sorry I couldn't match my boyfriend. I just wanna let y'all know that y'all look extra wack." I laughed and turned around in a circle. I had on a grey and black fitted sweater with a hood, and a pair of black pants and gray and black pumps. I wore my black coach messenger bag over my shoulder and spiral curled my hair all over. I was doin' it up today.

As we proceeded to the auditorium, we ran into Kristen who we could hardly recognize.

"Girl, you dyed your hair! It's cute!" I said, playing in her hair.

Kristen had finally taken out the red and dyed her hair auburn. It was calm but cute. She wore a blue jean skirt, brown heels, and a brown top; it was a really cute outfit. I was proud of my cousin.

"What made you change your hair?" Monique asked.

"I was at the beauty shop, so instead of her dying it blond, I told her to use auburn."

Monique made the ugliest face I had ever seen. "Thank God you didn't dye it blond, 'cause I would've had to tell you about yourself." We all laughed and proceeded to the gym. The show was about to start.

"Did you grab a program?" I asked Kristen.

"Yeah, IRS is first, and then—"

"They put IRS first? That's weird; they probably gonna get the crowd poppin'."

"That's alright," Monique commented. Everybody knew she was in love with COPPA. He was cute, light skinned and short, and was a pretty good rapper. He was silly, but I liked laughing at his jokes.

"Girl, ain't nobody thinkin' about no COPPA," Kristen said, laughing.

"Whateva. That's my boo. Now be quiet, they about to come on." All four of the guys came on the stage whilin' out. They threw towels in the audience and had everybody on their feet.

"When I say IR you say S. IR—"

"S!"

"IR!"

"S!"

They were hype; nobody was booing them off the stage no time soon. The next act was a group from CMA high School. They seemed like they were gonna tear it up, but one of the guys came out looking scared. The music came on and, at first, they were horrible, then when the music came on, and two of them started dancin', I got excited.

"Go y'all!" I screamed from the twelfth row.

"They can't hear you, and besides, Community Tech's Most Wanted is better than them," said Monique.

"But that's alright, 'cause that one light-skinned dude in the front is cute," Kristen commented. I sat down at Kristen's comment and looked at the program.

"Who's next?" Monique asked.

"ANLU."

"Well, I'm 'bout to go get a drink of water. Call me when they finish freakin' the floor down." Kristen was a mess.

"They aren't that bad. Everybody freaks the floor down, and you wasn't sayin' that when FON was on the stage. What does that stand for, anyway?

"Freaks of Nature and get it right!" She threw her hands up like she was about to fight.

"You don't know none of them, so please get off their jock." I laughed and gave Monique a five for her comment. After a couple more acts, Community Tech's Most Wanted came on.

"I might not be able to stay for the whole thing; they are some freaks," I told Monique.

"Yeah," Kristen added.

"I might be walking out with you." The boys came on the stage dancing like usual, and then all of a sudden, all we saw were towels. One boy walked down to the front of the stage and just stood there.

"Girl, I have to go." I tried to climb over Monique.

"But, wait, they're almost done."

By the time I got over her, Kristen was behind me. As I got to the hallway, I heard a big scream from all the girls in the audience. I didn't even want to look back. Shoot, with everything going on in there, I might turn into salt.

I grabbed my pop and chips and met Kristen back by the door. She was peeking in periodically to see if it was okay. "How does it look in there?" I asked, opening a bag of Cheetos.

"It's the fashion show part. They got a whole bunch of girls up there with prom dresses, modeling. Not really of any interest to me." I stood in the doorway watching the girls walk down the runway with guys dressed up in all white suits.

"Here comes your girl." Kristen turned around and looked at me.

"Who? Ain't no girl of mine up there." I looked closer and I saw Shayla Thompson in the cutest dress I had ever seen.

"That dress is tight, though," Kristen commented, leaning against the door and folding her arms.

"That dress is sweet. I wonder where they got it from?" Shayla just rubbed me the wrong way sometimes. One day she was cool, then the next she was all in James' face and lookin' at me all funny. She was pretty, smart, and one of the most popular girls in school, but she wasn't right. She was mean to everybody and she gossiped too much, and that's what made her unattractive.

"You want to go back in?" Just as I made that comment the lights came up and everybody came out of the auditorium. Kristen and I scooted back and waited for Monique to meet us in the hallway.

"Hey, y'all, Eric and 'dem want to go out to eat. Y'all wanna go?"

"I thought you weren't talking to Eric?" Kristen commented.

"We still cool as friends, but that boyfriend/girlfriend stuff is not happenin'. So do y'all wanna go or not?"

"Naw, I got dance class tonight, and I have to catch up on some homework." Monique seemed to not care.

"Kristen, you wanna go?"

"Yeah, I'll go. Who else is going?"

"Eric, Alonzo, James, me, you, and two other girls I don't know."

"I'll look out for James, 'cause I have a feeling who those two other girls are," Kristen whispered.

"Thanks," I said, laughing. "And take Nakiya wit' you, 'cause I don't want you sittin' there by yourself." Kristen turned around and smiled. I headed toward the front door. I hoped my mom was coming to get me. It was only 5:00, but by my dance class being at seven, I knew I wouldn't have been able to hang out like I wanted and still be on time for dance class. I sat outside the school watching all the kids get picked up by their parents, ride home with their friends, or walk to the bus stop. All of us were getting older, growing up, and being independent. Half the kids that walked out, I remembered from elementary, and just to see them now is incredible. God does take care of his own, even though we may not realize it.

My mom pulled up seconds later and I ran and jumped in the car. She smiled as I slid in the seats and threw my book bag in the back seat.

"How was school, Honey?"

"It was so good, Mom, and God is good." I turned around, put on my seatbelt, and sat back, thinking about God's goodness. He was so sweet to me.

CHAPTER 25

Kiva, your feet are wrong. I need your kicks to be higher and your arms to be more relaxed. What are you doing?" Mrs. Nabbit was getting on my nerves. She knew that I hated ballet and that I wanted to be in the modern piece, but she wanted to push me to do something I hadn't already mastered, and now she sees how much I suck. She probably wants to change her mind now.

"Alright Ladies, let's try it again. And 5,6,7,8 and up and kick and up and kick, puede bu re and peke, peke, peke, turn leap, turn leap, turn leap, sashay switch leap." She stopped us. "I need to see you ladies one at a time, because something is not looking right." Oh great. I know what's not looking right, me. There were only five of us in this dance; why did we have to do it one at a time? Mrs. Nabbit walked back and forth, rubbing her head.

"Ladies, the show is next week, and we need to get this together. You are the International Company; you have traveled all over dancing for everybody else. Now when it's time to dance for your friends and family here, you want to look sloppy. I won't have it, and I will pull people if you don't get it together."

Everybody looked at each other, shocked that she was so angry.

"Kiva, let me see you first," Mrs. Nabbit asked calmly.

"Father God," I whispered, "please give me the strength, and bring the moves back to my remembrance."

"C'mon, Kiva, we don't have all day!"

"And 5, 6, 7, 8 and up and kick and up and kick and puede bu re and peke, peke, peke, turn leap, turn leap, turn leap, sashay switch leap." I stopped in perfect position after finishing my move. Mrs. Nabbit paused and walked over to me.

"That was fine, but I need your arms to be neater. I want you in the front." Finally I got it right. Thank you, Jesus, because if I had to do that again by myself, I was gonna fall out. I guess that's what I get for not doing the move full out in the first place. My bad.

Class lasted about twenty more minutes, then we grabbed water bottles and towels, talked for a few minutes, and left.

I got home, jumped in the shower and jumped out 20 minutes later. The water felt so good, I wanted to stay in longer, but I didn't want to come out lookin' like a prune. I grabbed my towel and ran into my room. The lotion against my skin was so cold, and I had to rub my hands together to warm it up. I threw on a sweatshirt and some jogging pants and pulled out my Bible. It was time to get into my word.

"Alright, Lord, what do I want to learn about today?" I said.

"Let's see, how about friends." I flipped to the back of my Bible and looked up the word "friend" in my concordance. I pulled out my notebook from under my bed, grabbed a pen from my dresser, and wrote down all the verses under friend.

"Proverbs 17:17, Proverbs 18:24, and Ecclesiastes 4:9-12; I'll look at these three verses first." I read them out loud.

"*A friend loves at all times, and a brother is born for adversity.*" I read it again and tried to understand its meaning in my life.

"Well, if my friend is going through something, or even has a problem, I shouldn't judge, look down upon, or anger my friend with my comments. I should love him despite. So no matter what problems come my friend's way, I should always be a safe haven they can come to so that they shall feel secure." I went to the next scripture and read it aloud.

"*A man of many companions may come to ruin, but there is a friend that sticks closer than a brother.*" As I began to ponder on the scripture, I thought about how few friends I had. I really only had three or four, and for some reason, it didn't bother me. I wasn't the most popular, and I was fine with that. I didn't have the most expensive clothes or a car, but God was still there for me, taking care of me and watching over me. I didn't have to worry about money or food or grades because as I followed God, my blessings followed me. So pretty much having a whole bunch of friends isn't all it's cracked up to be 'cause if you don't have Jesus, then you're not complete.

I went to the final verse in Ecclesiastes; it read, *"Two are better than one, because they have a good return for their work: If one falls down, his friend can help him up. But pity the man who falls and has no one to help him up!"* I didn't even know there were verses about having friends in the Bible. I understood perfectly and knew that God wanted us to have friends, and that he has ordained people to be in our lives, but we have to stop hanging around those people who aren't any good for us and start pressing toward what God has for us, because it's much better. I prayed for about an hour and then realized it was ten o'clock. I laid in my bed thinking about how good God was and turned over when the phone rang.

"Hello."

"Hey, Kiva, you sleep?"

"I was about to, wassup." I rolled over on my side.

"Well, I wanted to talk to you about us going to two different schools." I guess he was finally ready to talk about it.

"I'm listening."

"Well, Baby I know that you were upset that I decided to go to Columbia instead of being closer to you, but I really feel led to go to New York." I sat up in the bed and tried to not get emotional.

"Kiva, but please be assured that just as focused as I am about being successful and fulfilling my purpose in life, I am just as focused on making sure you are happy, and supplying all your needs."

He always knew what to say to make me melt.

"James, initially it did hurt, but I understand, and I know that God will see us through."

You are my one, Sweetheart."

"You're my one, too, Babe."

"Let's pray."

CHAPTER 26

Alright, Kiva, wash those dishes and iron out your clothes for tomorrow, TGIF."

My mother walked into the living room and sat next to my father. It was Thursday already and the week just flew by. Thursdays were usually hectic, but I didn't have dance class today, thank God. I used to think that my parents had it easy, shoot, being grown is worse than being a kid. Work, work, and then come home and work more on your family. So sometimes I don't mind doing the dishes, or whatever chores I have to do before it's time to go to bed, because I knew that God had blessed me with two of the most loving, giving, unselfish parents in the world, and I couldn't do enough chores to thank God for that.

It was almost eleven, and I was tired. As I plopped on the bed, my cell phone rang.

"Hello."

"Hello, uh, can I speak to Kiva?"

"This is she. Who is this?"

"Alex."

I paused and was trying to decide whether I should hang up, or pop off on him.

"Wassup, Alex, what did you want." I figured I would tolerate him for a little bit, just to see if he apologized.

"I'm cool, just wanted to holla at ya. How come you don't call me no more?"

"Alex, you know why, I don't even know why you actin' brand new." Alex laughed.

"Look Baby, I want to apologize for getting your little boyfriend's panties all in a bunch, you gotta admit it was funny though, tryin' to defend his little girlfriend."

I rolled my eyes.

"I accept your apology, did you need anything else."

"Ooooh, Kiva, I see you got a little feistiness in you."

"Alex, I have to go, I need to get to bed."

"So, how is your dad doin, he was real cool." Why was he trying to keep me on the phone?

"He is good Alex, anything else?" I was ready to hang up at this point.

"Aye, what church you go to?" I was shocked he even asked.

"I go to Perfecting Faith, where do you go to church?"

"Oh, I don't go to church. I don't understand it, you know. I'm kind of in between Buddhism and Christianity right now." A black Buddhist in Detroit; I never heard of it.

"Why Buddhism? What's wrong with Christianity?" By this time I sat up in my bed.

"It's too many hypocrites, the same people that's in the church are the same people at the club tryin' to get in free before ten. And don't tell me not to have sex, when you married and you don't know what I have to go through every day. I'm just tired of the hypocrites." He was angry, but I was about to let him know what the deal was, because he was clearly misinformed.

"Alex, you have to get your salvation no matter what others are doing. You either goin' to church with the hypocrites, or goin' to hell with them, so you might as well take the high road. I feel you, though, on the sexual aspect, but we all have to go through it. If you get into your word for yourself, then you can learn a lot. The thing with Christianity is you won't end up being the same thing you were when you first gave your life to Christ. He wants to perfect you, and the only way he can do that is if you give yourself to him wholeheartedly to use."

Alex was quiet, pondering what I just said.

"Yeah, but I don't know if I'm ready for all that."

"Well, it's your choice, but just remember that Jesus had a choice to die for our sins and let us be free. He made that choice for you, not for himself, so you should think about not thinking about yourself. Believe me, it's worth it."

The phone was silent.

"Hey, why don't you come to my church Sunday; my dad's preaching."

"I don't know about all that, I'm goin' out Saturday, so I might be asleep."

"Well, if you want to come, the door is always open. Do you know where it is?"

"Yeah, I know where it is. I'll see, but I ain't makin' no promises."

"That's cool, but just remember, the door is open." We got off the phone and I just thanked God for using me at that moment. I could tell that Alex really needed to hear that, and even if he doesn't come Sunday, he'll come someday.

✝✝✝✝✝

"Hallelujah in the sanctuary, Hallelujah, we give him the Glory..." The choir was off the hook this morning. They had the little kids sing this Sunday and they were jammin'. My mom decided to sit closer so she could see my dad, and me and my brother sat in the middle. I wanted to look presentable, so I gave myself a genie ponytail and put on a black skirt that flared out at the bottom and a long-sleeved blouse. It buttoned up in the front and was really cute. My brother wore a suit and put on his gators.

"Good afternoon saints, you may have a seat. This Sunday, Pastor Grayson won't be here, but if you know my pastor like I know my pastor, you know he won't let just anybody up in this pulpit. Can I get an Amen!

"Amen!"

"So this Sunday, our own Minister Niran will be edifying us with God's words. We thank God for him." People clapped as my father walked up to the podium. When I turned around, I saw Alex walk through the door. You could tell he just threw on whatever he wanted, but that was okay, he came, and that's what mattered.

"Thank you, God." I said, looking up.

"Congregation, I just want to talk to y'all today about love. The greatest commandment was based on love, if it had not been for God lovin' each and everyone of us, where would we be?"

Daddy was preachin' up a storm. By the middle of the sermon, people were standin' up and praisin' God for everything he had done. My church was the best place for me, and I'm glad I wasn't going too far for school. I knew that God was everywhere, but I needed this church and I needed to be tied to this ministry, it was so powerful, it moved me, and it was for God and by God. Near the end of his sermon, people were in the aisles, on the floor, and waving their hands toward heaven. I turned around and saw Alex standing up reverencing God but not moving, just staring at the pulpit.

"God, I know you have a plan for his life; he has so much to offer and can bring joy to others lives in whatever gift you have for him, so God, do a work in him like no other, turn his life around, and show him who he is in Christ."

As I prayed, I saw the tears roll down his face and his head fall down to the ground. He couldn't hold it in anymore. All the lying, cheating, and stealing wasn't for him. He knew he had to give it up, and you could see freedom being given to him through his release of all the sin. His hands went up and his face stayed toward the ground. I couldn't believe it, God was moving right before my eyes. I looked toward heaven as the tears fell and felt him stir up my spirit. He was in this place. I threw my arms up and opened my mouth to praise him. "Thank you Jesus; thank you, Jesus!"

CHAPTER 27

Kiva, oh my goodness, it is the last day of high school for us, can you believe it!" Monique stuffed a chip in her mouth and sat back in her chair. We were eating our last lunch together as high school seniors. This year had been a rough one for me, but I think I was more nervous about being away from my friends and family. Kristen was going to still be in high school, Monique was going to Michigan State, Ananda would be at the University of Michigan, and of course James, my beloved boo, would be all the way in New York.

"You know what Monique, I am so excited for this summer and going to college, but I am really going to miss you." She started to tear up, and I was holding back my tears.

"Oh, Kiva, I love you too, but we will see each other, I'll call you all the time."

"I'll call you all the time too!" We both hugged each other, and in the midst of our sentimental moment, we bursted into laughter.

"Kiva, so what are you and James gonna do?" I was hoping she didn't ask me. Everytime I thought about my bestfriend moving all the way to New York and me possibly not seeing him until next summer made me sad.

'Well, we're gonna try to make it work. He said that he wants to make it work, and I have faith in him, and our relationship. Hey. My parents did it, so why can't we." I tried to hold back the disappointment and fear that I held onto, but I knew Monique could see it, she knew me to well.

"Mmm, so you aren't worried that Shawny will be at NYU?" I knew she was fishing for the truth from me, but I didn't want to verbally share that with her, at least not yet, we still had the whole summer to make memories.

"Girl, I'm not thinking about her, and neither is James. That chapter is closed."

Monique looked at me in disbelief and quickly changed the subject.

"Well, let's go to this last class girl, last class of the school year."

"I know right."

We walked into Mr. Smith's class, and it was a zoo. People were sitting on desks, a group of guys were rapping in the corner, and some students were even drawing on the chalkboard.

"Where is Mr. Smith?" Monique asked one of the people writing on the chalk board.

"Oh girl, he went to the principal's office. He told us as long as we didn't make too much noise, we would be good."

Wow, this was it huh.

"Monique and I found a quiet corner in the back of the classroom and chatted until the bell rang. By the time we got to our lockers, James was already there, waiting for me.

"Hey Baby."

"Hey, James, how are you?" I felt like I hadn't seen him all day. He looked as good as the first day I met him four years ago. Tall, caramel, and handsome.

"Can I give you a ride home?"

"Definitely."

"Are you excited for the summer, Kiva?" He opened my door for me and threw his bookbag in the backseat.

"I am Babe, we have about two months to really spend a lot of time together."

I could see the slight sadness in his eyes from him knowing I was disappointed in him leaving.

"Kiva, you can come visit me whenever you're on break, and I'll be home for the holidays." It wasn't making it any better, but I appreciated the effort.

"James, it's okay, we will be okay. I love you and you love me. We are going to make this work, and when the time is right, we will be in the same state together. Plus, if you cheat on me, I'll cut you."

He looked at me and smirked.

"Baby, you are the only person I want to be with, no one else."

We ended up in front of my house so quick, I didn't want to get out of the car. It wasn't like he was leaving tomorrow, but I knew in my heart this was going to be the last time he drove me home from school, our school, where we first met. This would be the last time that I had the security in knowing that I would see him tomorrow, at my locker, waiting for me after lunch, or being able to cheer for him at the basketball games. As I looked out the window, tears started to fall. I knew that there was a slight chance, that after this summer, we may grow apart, and that slight chance, really hurt.

"Kiva, Baby don't cry."

He put his arms around me, and I came closer to him.

"James, I don't want you to go, I love you so much." James rubbed my arm and sat me up in the car.

"Kiva, I understand how you feel, but this isn't all about me." I looked at him confused.

"Kiva, you are going to be at Oakland all by yourself, and you are scared. You're so used to having someone around you. Monique, Kristen, and Ananda are always around, and now you have to face the world on your own, and you don't like that do you?" I wiped my eyes and nodded.

"Kiva, it's apart of growing up Baby. Besides, this will help you to become independent, and stand on your own two feet. It's gonna be okay Baby, where is your faith."

He was right but I still wanted to have a pity party. No one was going to be there for me, no one I knew at least. I had to start all over and I wasn't too happy about that. He tickled my stomach and got me to laugh. I was being emotional, but that was me, a big ball of emotions.

"James, I know, you're right, whatever." I pushed him off of me and he smirked.

"So, since this is our last summer together, what are we going to do to make it memorable?" I put my arms around him and kissed him on the cheek.

"Kiva, we're gonna enjoy every moment, and make memories that last a lifetime."

At that moment, in that second, I knew in my heart that James and I were gonna be together forever.

www.ingramcontent.com/pod-product-compliance
Lightning Source LLC
Chambersburg PA
CBHW020422180626
46812CB00003B/1105